Sin, Sex & the CIA

by Michael Parker
&
Susan Parker

A SAMUEL FRENCH ACTING EDITION

SAMUEL FRENCH

FOUNDED 1830

NEW YORK HOLLYWOOD LONDON TORONTO

SAMUELFRENCH.COM

MUSIC USE NOTE

IMPORTANT BILLING AND CREDIT REQUIREMENTS

Sin, Sex & the CIA

by

MICHAEL PARKER

was first produced at the

Lemon Bay Playhouse

in Englewood, Florida on August 15th, 2006.

Cast:

Luke James	Jim Walsh
Daniel Warren	Lawrence C. Richardson
Margaret Johnson	Judy "JJ" Juliano
Rev. Samuel Abernathy	Vince Delgato
Millicent	Michelle Neitzel
Heather Ann Farady	Liz Krupa
Ranger Don	Cael Barkman

Directed by Michael Parker and Susan Parker

Designed by Mary Lou Ardrey

CHARACTERS

LUKE JAMES (Age 25-30) A CIA agent on his first field assignment. We are left to wonder how he ever got the job. He gets caught in his own booby traps, he walks into walls, he sets fire to the kitchen, he gets a bucket stuck on his head, etc. In short, if there's a wrong way to do something, he'll find it! He continues to repeat throughout the play, "I can do that!" but, in fact, as Margaret says, "He really can't do anything." *(Likeable, enthusiastic, hopelessly incompetent)*

DANIEL WARREN (Age 50-60) Daniel introduces himself as a retired Marine Corps Sergeant. In fact, he is a mercenary hired by OPEC. He is "all business," and quickly realizes how easily he can handle Luke James. Possessing a sharp southern wit, he is never at a loss for words, especially when he repeatedly catches the Reverend Samuel Abernathy in compromising situations. Pursued relentlessly by Margaret, he manages to remain professional, and complete his assignment. *(Competent, a "tough guy" with a quick, dry wit)*

MARGARET JOHNSON (Age 35-55) An Assistant Secretary of State. She is a professional, and, as we would expect, good at her job. However, it is the other side of Margaret, which brings her character to life. She appears to be run by her libido. Never subtle, Margaret relentlessly pursues Daniel throughout the play. Despite his repeated rejections, she will not take no for an answer. Ever resourceful, she continually finds new ways to entice him into her bed. *(Attractive, determined, a "sexual predator")*

THE REVEREND SAMUEL ABERNATHY (Age 50-60) A quintessential television evangelist, complete with white linen suit and pompadour hairstyle. He tends to "talk down" to people and is constantly preaching. Eventually however, we see he does not always practice what he preaches. Throughout the play, he constantly misinterprets everything he sees and hears, until finally, he is left totally and thoroughly confused, and presents himself as a rather pathetic figure. *(Arrogant, bombastic, but nevertheless, sincere in his beliefs)*

MILLICENT (Age 25-30) The Reverend Samuel Abernathy's secretary. She is correctly referred to by Samuel as "an innocent." She is dowdy and unglamorous, in fact, "a plain Jane," who makes no attempt to improve her appearance. It is only when she finds herself attracted to Luke, that we see, what is perhaps the real Millicent. After taking a seduction lesson from Heather, she emerges from her shell, in one of the plays most hilarious scenes. (Shy, frumpy, compassionate, then finally, "a bombshell")

HEATHER ANN FARADAY (Age 30-35) Introduces herself as the neighbor from the next cabin, but she is, in fact, Daniel's partner and fellow OPEC agent. She plays the "role" of the Chagos Islands Representative with competence and a great deal of panache. Although a mercenary, she shows a kind and sympathetic side when Millicent asks her for help. *(Glamorous, sexy, smart, with a great sense of humor)*

RANGER DON (Any age) Is, in fact, Donna Yarid, the real representative of the Chagos Islands, disguised as a man. A brief role, but one, which at the very end of the play, holds the key to the entire plot. *(Unassuming, competent and business-like)*

SETTING

A CIA safe house, somewhere in the mountains of Virginia

TIME

The present
Early Friday evening

ACT I

The curtain rises on an empty set. It is the interior of a log cabin. D.R. is a bar or drinks table with bottles, glasses etc. Above this is the door to bedroom 2, and above that the door to bedroom 1. D.L. is a stone fireplace. The fire may be lit. Above this is the door to bedroom 3. There's a bearskin rug on the floor U.R. of the couch. U.S.C. is the front door with a window on each side with draperies, which are open. These windows should open by sliding up the lower panel. U.S.L. is a door to the bathroom and U.S.R. leads off to the kitchen.

On the U.S. wall, between the left window and the front door, is a combination umbrella and coat stand. D.S. is a couch and coffee table with a low back chair on each side. The furniture is angled towards the fireplace. The furnishings are rustic and the decor very much "upscale" log cabin, a painting or two, perhaps a deer head or antique gun rack etc.

The stage is dimly lit and we see a flashlight shining through the windows. After a moment or two, the L. window slides up and LUKE JAMES creeps furtively in and strikes a karate pose. (Age perhaps 25-30, he is a CIA agent and, as we shall see, not very good at his job. However, what he lacks in experience and expertise, he makes up for in enthusiasm. He is wearing a raincoat over a dress shirt and tan pants. He continues to flash the light around the stage. Seeing no one, he reaches out the window and lifts in an enormous suitcase. He locates the light switch by the front door, switches it on, takes off his raincoat and hangs it on the coat stand, and then opens the suitcase. He produces an electronic scanner, which he switches on. He then moves slowly around the room and backs right toward the kitchen door as DANIEL WARREN enters from the kitchen to watch. DANIEL, perhaps age 55, presents himself as a former U.S. Marine Corps Sergeant, who is employed by the CIA as a replacement for the regular live-in safe-house caretaker. He is, in fact, a free-lance mercenary hired by OPEC to disrupt and prevent the meeting, which is to take place this evening in the safe house. He is a solid, down to earth individual, a little rough around the edges, and not impressed by CIA agents in general, and Luke James in particular. He is wearing boots, blue jeans and a denim shirt.

As LUKE backs R. in front of DANIEL, he turns suddenly D.S. and then continues D.R., never seeing DANIEL who follows him D.R. and eventually taps him on the shoulder. LUKE, startled, tries to adopt a karate pose, but DANIEL holds him off by placing one hand on his head and takes his legs right out from under him. DANIEL then places a large boot across LUKE's back.

DANIEL. Who are you?

LUKE. Who are you?

DANIEL. Listen buddy, I've got another foot and I can put it in a much more painful place if you don't answer my question.

LUKE. I'm Luke James.

DANIEL. *(Not removing his foot.)* Well, Mr. Luke James, perhaps you'd better tell me what you're doing here.

LUKE. I'm sweeping for electronic bugs.

DANIEL. Why?

LUKE. I've been assigned to this house this weekend.

DANIEL. Assigned by whom?

LUKE. You know. *(Pause.)* The Firm.

DANIEL. *(Removing his foot and rolling his eyes.)* Oh Lord, another agent. *(LUKE gets up.)* Let's see some ID. *(LUKE takes an ID out of his wallet.)* How long have you been working for the CIA?

LUKE. Actually, this is my first field assignment. *(Hands him his ID card.)* Who are you?

DANIEL. I'm Daniel Warren, U.S. Marine Corps, retired. Mr. Cole the regular caretaker of this safe house had some chest pains this morning and they took him in for medical tests. They called me to take his place. Why don't you brief me on this weekend.

LUKE. There is a very important meeting tonight, here in this house, between the U.S. State Department and a representative of the Chagos Islands.

DANIEL. The what?

LUKE. The Chagos Islands. They are a vast archipelago stretching across hundreds of square miles in the Indian Ocean. Recent geological studies have established that this island group is sitting on more oil than any other country on the planet, except Saudi Arabia. OPEC is pressuring the Chagosians to join the cartel. The Chagosians have indicated some interest in placing themselves under the protectorate of the United States. The meeting this weekend is to negotiate the terms. As you can imagine, OPEC will stop at nothing to prevent this from happening. It could even mean the downfall and breakup of the cartel.

DANIEL. And they sent you?

LUKE. I can assure you I am a highly trained security expert. It is my job to secure this cabin for the meeting tonight.

DANIEL. O.K. What's the timetable?

LUKE. I don't know. Details of the meeting have been kept so secret we do not even know who this representative is, or even when he, or she, will arrive. However, the U.S. State Department representative will be arriving shortly. It is my job to keep any potential intruders away.

DANIEL. Just how do you plan to do that?

LUKE. I have everything I need right here in my FARTAD.

(He walks to his suitcase and puts the electrical equipment away.)

DANIEL. What?

LUKE. My FARTAD.

DANIEL. Your what?

LUKE. F.A.R.T.A.D. Field Agents Restrictive Techniques And Devices. *(DANIEL shakes his head.)* Do not use the front door!

DANIEL. Why not?

LUKE. It's booby-trapped.

DANIEL. It's what?

LUKE. It's booby-trapped with a giant cargo net. Anyone trying to gain entry through the front door will be trapped. I have also rigged up what we in the trade, call alley-oop cables outside each of the windows.

DANIEL. Alley-oop?

LUKE. Anyone approaching the window will step into a loop of rope, which will, with a series of weights and pulleys, haul them upside down into the air, alley-oop! *(A car is heard pulling up outside.)* That's a car.

DANIEL. No kidding!

LUKE. Stand still. Leave it to me.

(LUKE rushes out the front door; there is a sudden noise, and a yell from LUKE. DANIEL raises his eyes heavenward and exits the front door. He returns immediately dragging LUKE behind him. A large mesh net covers LUKE. He struggles ferociously as he lashes out with karate moves. DANIEL tries to help, but he gets entangled in the net, and they both go down as MARGARET JOHNSON enters through the front door.

MARGARET, age perhaps 35-55, is employed as one of the many assistants to the Secretary of State. A competent career oriented woman, she will, as we shall see, soon reveal another side of herself, that of an aggressive man-hunter. She is wearing a long raincoat, over an attractive tailored suit. She carries with her a purse and an umbrella. The raincoat is wet, and we see it is now raining outside. With her back to the room, she closes her umbrella, puts it in the umbrella stand, closes the front door, and turns to watch DANIEL and LUKE struggling in the net. Eventually DANIEL frees himself and stands up. LUKE, still in the net, stands up and does his karate moves, as DANIEL and MAR-GARET watch.)

MARGARET. Hello.

DANIEL. Good evening madam. May I ask who you are?

MARGARET. I'm Margaret Johnson from the U.S. State Department.

DANIEL. Welcome. I'm Daniel Warren, caretaker of this safe house. *(He pauses as they watch the continuing struggles of LUKE inside the net.)* And this is Luke James from the Complete

Idiots Academy.
 MARGARET. The what?
 DANIEL. The CIA.

(LUKE frees himself from the net, stands up, and bundles up the net.)

DANIEL. Luke, this is Margaret Johnson from the State Department.
 MARGARET. Hello

(LUKE moves U.S. and shakes hands with her.)

LUKE. Hello, sorry about that, I was just testing one of the booby-traps.
 DANIEL. *(Rolls his eyes and turns to LUKE.)* Well?
 LUKE. Well what?
 DANIEL. Don't you think you ought to check her security ID?
 LUKE. Right, yes, good idea, I can do that. *(He looks at MARGARET.)* ID please madam? (*MARGARET reaches into her purse and produces a security ID card.*) Right, everything looks good. Thank you.

(He hands the card back to MARGARET who returns it to her purse, as LUKE returns the cargo net to his FARTAD.)

DANIEL. Let me take your coat.

(MARGARET hands him her coat. DANIEL hangs Margaret's coat on the coat stand.)

MARGARET. Thank you. Does he know what he's doing?

DANIEL. I don't think he can do anything. Would you like some coffee?

MARGARET. Thank you. *(DANIEL exits to the kitchen.)* Now, tell me what do you know about the meeting this evening?

(She comes D. to sit on couch L. side.)

LUKE. *(Moves to the R. chair.)* Not much. Only that it's very hush-hush, and my job is to keep out any potential intruders.

MARGARET. That's right, it's been kept so secret that I don't even know who the Chagos Islands' representative is. They wouldn't say whom they were sending. I don't even know if it's a man or a woman. Incidentally, I was told that the caretaker's name was Christopher Cole, not Daniel Warren.

LUKE. Ah yes, well, you see Mr. Cole had to go for some medical tests, and they sent Daniel to take his place.

MARGARET. Did you check his ID?

LUKE. Ah yes, well, er…no.

MARGARET. Maybe Mr. Warren was right about the Complete Idiots Academy.

LUKE. What?

MARGARET. Nothing. Don't you think you should check him out?

LUKE. Right, good idea, I can do that. I'll have to use my cell phone to speed dial headquarters. There are never any phones in safe houses. It eliminates the bugging problem.

(He moves R. and starts to dial.
DANIEL enters from the kitchen carrying a tray with mugs, cof-

fee pot, etc. He comes D. As he passes LUKE, LUKE turns away attempting to hide the fact that he is using his cell phone. DANIEL looks at LUKE, shrugs, then places the tray on the coffee table and sits on the sofa R. side.)

DANIEL Here we are.

MARGARET. Thank you. *(To LUKE.)* Well?

LUKE. It's no good, I can't get through, must be interference from the storm.

(As DANIEL pours the coffee, and hands out mugs, MARGARET tries to attract LUKE's attention by jerking her head in DANIEL'S direction.)

MARGARET. Daniel, I believe Mr. James has something to ask you.

LUKE. I do? *(MARGARET looks at him.)* Oh yes, right. *(He moves to the R. end of the sofa.)* I think perhaps we'd better see some ID, Mr. Warren.

DANIEL. Certainly.

(He pulls out his driver's license from his shirt pocket.)

LUKE. Well, that seems to be in order.

MARGARET. What type of ID is that?

LUKE. It's his driver's license. *(Shows it to MARGARET.)* Look, Daniel Warren and his photo.

MARGARET. And his security ID?

LUKE. Ah yes, right. *(To DANIEL.)* And your security ID?

DANIEL. I'm afraid I left it behind when I got the emergency call to report here.

LUKE. Oh, I see.

(He hands Daniel's ID back to him.)

MARGARET. Oh, I see? That's it?

LUKE. That's what?

MARGARET. Never mind, I'll talk to you later.

LUKE. *(Returns to the chair.)* What I don't understand is how we're supposed to know who the Chagos Islands' representative is when we meet him.

MARGARET. Or her, don't forget, it could be a woman.

LUKE. Either way, how will we know?

MARGARET. There's a recognition code word.

LUKE. Don't you think I ought to know what it is?

MARGARET. Certainly, it's—

(LUKE leaps to his feet, puts his hand up to stop her, looks furtively around the room, then signals to MARGARET to follow him R to the door of bedroom 2. She does, leaving her purse on the couch.)

LUKE. Now whisper.

(MARGARET whispers in his ear.)

LUKE. *(In a loud voice.)* The cook is awake! What sort of code word is that?

MARGARET. One that he *(Points to DANIEL)* now knows. Well, the damage is done; let's just hope he checks out.

DANIEL. *(Stands and moves U.L.)* Don't worry about me, it doesn't matter whether I know the code word or not. *(Looks out window.)* It's really coming down now, looks like we're in for a bad storm.

MARGARET. Oh dear, I left my bags in the car.

LUKE. Your car! I need to set an alarm on it. I'll get your suitcase. May I have your keys?

(He moves U.S. to put on Margaret's raincoat as DANIEL comes D. and sits on the couch L. side.)

MARGARET. *(Crosses L. and gets her keys from her purse.)* Is an alarm really necessary?

LUKE. Be prepared, that's my motto. In any event it won't take a minute, I have everything ready and prepared in my FAR-TAD.

MARGARET. That's my coat, why don't you wear your own?

LUKE. Right, I can do that.

(He takes off Margaret's coat and puts on his own.)

MARGARET. Your FARTAD?

DANIEL. Don't ask.

LUKE. My FARTAD. F.A.R.T.A.D., field agents restrictive techniques and devices.

MARGARET. Here you are.

(She moves U.S. and hands the keys to LUKE.)

LUKE. Thank you. *(Picks up his FARTAD.)* I won't be long.

(He exits front door and closes it behind him.)

DANIEL. What can they be thinking about, sending us an idiot like that!

MARGARET. *(Comes D.L.)* I know what I'm thinking about.

DANIEL. What?

MARGARET. *(Now at the L. end of the couch.)* You!

DANIEL. Me?

MARGARET. Yes, you! *(Sits on the couch and runs her fingers down DANIEL's arm.)* You are just a great-looking guy.

(DANIEL stands and escapes R., MARGARET follows.)

DANIEL. Madam, what I am, is a retired U.S. Marine Corps Sergeant with a job to do. Under normal circumstances, I would love to be called a great-looking guy, especially by a beautiful woman like you. Maybe later we can continue this conversation, but for now, we both have a job to do.

(She stands and advances R. towards DANIEL.)

MARGARET. Oh, so you do find me attractive?

(She runs her fingers up his chest.)

DANIEL. *(Takes a few steps backwards.)* As I said, we have a job to do.

MARGARET. *(Continues to advance on him.)* Well, later is good, but now is better.

(She flings her arms around him and kisses him passionately full

on the lips. After a second or two he pushes her away.)

DANIEL.. Excuse me madam, but this is neither the time nor the place.

(MARGARET sits on the arm of the R. chair, hitches up her skirt and crosses her legs provocatively.)

MARGARET. All right big boy, the place is my room and the time is later.

(LUKE enters through the front door with his FARTAD, and Margaret's suitcase. He sets the bags down by the door and closes the door behind him. MARGARET rearranges her skirt and sits properly in the chair. LUKE paces.)

LUKE. Operation car security is completed. Anyone attempting to infiltrate the vehicle by touching the car will be greeted with a siren, and exploding paint balls, which I have carefully concealed in the door handles. So, do not attempt to enter your car without informing me so that I can deactivate the alarm system.

MARGARET. That's fine, but my briefcase is on the front seat, and I'll need it for the meeting tonight.

LUKE. Right, I'll go get it.

(He exits front door.)

MARGARET. Where were we? *(Hitches up her skirt again and strikes a provocative pose.)* Oh yes, my room and later. By the way big boy, which is my room?

(She advances on DANIEL. He backs away U.R., picks up her suitcase and holds it between them like a shield.)

DANIEL. *(Backing left toward bedroom 3.)* You never give up do you. You could have been a great Marine.

MARGARET. *(Still advancing.)* I would prefer the Mounties.

DANIEL. Why?

MARGARET. They always get their man.

DANIEL. *(Now at the door of bedroom 3.)* There you see that's what I mean. This is your room ma'am.

(MARGARET crosses in front of DANIEL and glances into the room.)

MARGARET. Boy, this is small, *(Turns to DANIEL and strikes a sexy pose in the doorway.)* but there's definitely room for two, you big, strong, soldier boy.

(DANIEL quickly puts down the suitcase between them.)

DANIEL. Marine ma'am, marine.

(He retreats R.)

MARGARET. I didn't know marines ever retreated.

DANIEL. The Yalu River was a retreat ma'am, mine is a strategic withdrawal. I will, however look forward to seeing more of you later. *(MARGARET reacts.)* Let me rephrase that.

MARGARET. Well then, a truce till later big boy.

(There is a loud bang off stage, immediately followed by a 4 to 5

second siren. MARGARET and DANIEL look at each other; look at the audience, and then at the front door. The front door opens slowly and LUKE enters with his back to the audience. He carries Margaret's briefcase. He closes the door and turns rather sheepishly down stage. His raincoat is covered with bright orange paint and soaking wet, his hands are orange, and he has streaks of orange paint down his face where he has obviously tried to wipe away the rain.)

DANIEL. Not again.
MARGARET. What happened?

(LUKE moves D.L. a little.)

LUKE. There's nothing to get excited about, I just had a slight malfunction, but everything is under control.

(He hands DANIEL Margaret's briefcase.)

DANIEL. You call being covered with orange paint under control?
LUKE. Right, I'll go and clean up. I can do that.

(DANIEL puts her briefcase behind the couch.)

DANIEL. You can use the bathroom in my quarters off the kitchen.
LUKE. Thanks.

(He picks up his FARTAD and exits to the kitchen.)

MARGARET. Take your time. *(To DANIEL.)* Alone again lover boy.

(DANIEL places Margaret's suitcase between them.)

DANIEL. I've told you, I am not your lover boy.
MARGARET. *(Moves suitcase to her R.)* And I'm telling you, you will be.
DANIEL. We'll see.
MARGARET. Oh dear, so you're still continuing your strategic withdrawal?
DANIEL. Yes ma'am.
MARGARET. *(Moves R.)* Well then, I suppose I shall have to find a different plan of attack.
DANIEL. *(Backs away.)* Attack?

(She continues to move towards him.)

MARGARET. Let's just call it a forward movement, and boy have I got some moves for you.

(DANIEL is now backed up against the L. side of the couch. She pounces on him and flings her arms around his neck. He falls backwards over the L. end of the couch, she falls between his legs on top of him and smothers him with kisses.
Enter through the front door THE REVEREND SAMUEL ABER-NATHY. Age perhaps 50-60; he is the quintessential evangelical, hell and damnation preacher. However, as we shall see, he does not always live up to the standards, which he is so keen to preach to others. He carries an umbrella, and has a raincoat draped over his shoulders covering an all white

outfit: white shoes, socks, pants, jacket, silk shirt and tie. His graying hair is worn in a pompadour style. He steps into the room and closes the door. He puts his umbrella in the umbrella stand. He turns and sees MARGARET and DANIEL in a compromising position on the couch. He slides his raincoat off his shoulders and it falls to the floor. He then strides purposefully down to the back of the couch, arms outspread and palms up.)

SAMUEL. Witness the sins of the flesh. *(DANIEL and MARGARET freeze and stare up at him.)* Oh Lord, forgive me. A few moments ago, out in this terrible storm I doubted you. I asked, "Why me?" Why did my car have to break down on this dark and desolate road? Now I clearly see your purpose. You have sent me here to save these miserable sinners from their carnal desires and the pleasures of the flesh.

(MARGARET stands and moves above the couch L. side.)

MARGARET. Hello. I'm Margaret Johnson.
SAMUEL. Good evening. I am the Reverend Samuel Abernathy.

(They shake hands.)

DANIEL. *(Stands.)* And I am Daniel Warren and I need a drink.

(DANIEL crosses R. to the drinks table.)

SAMUEL. Just as I suspected. Sinners, sinners enjoying the

pleasures of the flesh, the pleasures of the flesh, without benefit of matrimony. Do you not know the retribution that awaits adulterers like you?

DANIEL. *(Pouring himself a drink.)* Hold on a minute. There really wasn't anything going on.

SAMUEL. Thank you Lord. Thank you. You brought me here just in time to rescue these two lost souls.

MARGARET. I'd hardly describe us as lost souls.

SAMUEL. Souls such as you are always lost, always searching. As the children of Israel searched for the Promised Land, so too are you searching. Have you found your promised land? I know I have.

MARGARET. *(To DANIEL.)* Ooh, can I lead you to your promised land?

SAMUEL. *(Glares at MARGARET and continues without missing a beat.)* Life you know is rather like a plate of beans. There are green beans and brown beans, wax beans and black beans, kidney beans, baked beans and even barbequed beans, but you know, when you've finished eating at the end of the day, they are all still just beans.

DANIEL. Would that make them "has beans"?

SAMUEL. *(Ignores DANIEL and continues.)* Although it is said variety is the spice of life, it is that very spice which can cause you heartache and despair. My poor, poor lost souls, do not be tempted down life's lost path, rather, travel as I do in an abundance of riches blessed by God.

DANIEL. What did he just say?

MARGARET. Absolutely nothing.

SAMUEL. Madam, it is my mission, my purpose, and my reason for being, that I find myself here to deliver you out of your sinful ways and onto the path of redemption.

DANIEL. *(Puts his glass down.)* I've heard quite enough. Reverend, it is my mission, my purpose and my reason for being here that I now require you to show me some ID.

(LUKE, now cleaned up, enters from the kitchen without his raincoat. He stops dead in his tracks and strikes a karate pose when he sees SAMUEL. He creeps D., unseen by SAMUEL.)

SAMUEL. Really, this is preposterous. I am known internationally for my ministry.

DANIEL. ID. Please. Now. *(Holds out his hand.)*

(SAMUEL reaches into his inside pocket and produces his wallet. LUKE is now immediately behind him and about to leap on him. SAMUEL takes a step to his R. to hand his ID to DANIEL. LUKE's leap is now into thin air, and he falls flat on the floor unconscious.)

SAMUEL. Very well, here it is. *(Hands DANIEL his ID.)* I left my secretary in the car down the road, and I must now bring her here to safety. But I want you to know I cannot condone your wanton ways, which I witnessed earlier. She is an innocent soul who must be protected from the evils of immoral activities. Therefore, as long as we are in this house, I do not expect to see any repetition of your licentious behavior. *(Sees LUKE.)* Who is this?

MARGARET. He's from the CIA.

SAMUEL. What?

DANIEL. *(Hands ID back to SAMUEL.)* Oh, not the Central Intelligence Agency, he's from the er—the—er—the other CIA, The Culinary Institute of America. He's the chef.

MARGARET. He is?

DANIEL. Yes, that's Mr. James, the chef.

SAMUEL. What is he doing on the floor?

MARGARET. He's—er—er—

DANIEL. He's asleep.

SAMUEL. What?

DANIEL. He's asleep.

SAMUEL. Why is he sleeping on the floor in the middle of the living room?

DANIEL. Well, er—er—

MARGARET. He suffers from narcolepsy.

DANIEL. He does?

MARGARET. Definitely. He falls asleep anywhere, all the time.

DANIEL. We now have a narcoleptic chef?

MARGARET. Absolutely.

SAMUEL. I will return shortly with my secretary. In the meantime perhaps you would be kind enough to phone Triple A. Here's my membership card. *(Removes a card from his wallet.)*

DANIEL. I'm afraid the only phone here is the chef's cell phone, and it doesn't appear to be working, probably because of the storm.

SAMUEL. *(Putting his card back in his wallet, moves L. to MARGARET.)* Oh dear. Madam, if it would not be too much of an imposition, do you think it would be possible for Millicent and myself to take shelter here until help can arrive?

MARGARET. Millicent?

SAMUEL. My secretary.

MARGARET. Well, I guess so. *(Glances at DANIEL who is frowning.)* At least until the phone is working and we can get some help.

SAMUEL. Of course. Thank you Ms. Johnson. *(He moves towards the front door, picks up his raincoat and turns with a flourish.)* Do not take advantage of my absence to continue your lascivious behavior. Remember, the Lord is watching you.

(SAMUEL picks up his umbrella and exits front door.)

DANIEL. *(Sits R. chair.)* Who or what is the Reverend Samuel Abernathy?

MARGARET. *(Sits L. couch.)* I don't know, but I get the feeling that if I was drowning he would be the first person to try to save my soul, while holding out an electric cattle prod.

(LUKE groans and staggers to his feet.)

LUKE. *(Strikes karate pose.)* Who was that? Where did he go?

DANIEL. He's the Reverend Samuel Abernathy. He went to get his secretary. Their car broke down and they'll be back in a few minutes.

MARGARET. Why don't you see if your phone is working and check him out.

LUKE. Yes, right. I can do that. I'm going to try headquarters in zone seven.

(LUKE takes out his cell phone and dials frantically.)

DANIEL. The only zone he'll reach is the twilight zone.
MARGARET. He does seem to be a little out of it.
DANIEL. He's never been in it.
MARGARET. *(To LUKE.)* Well?

LUKE. Nothing.

MARGARET. *(Sits on sofa L. end.)* Then we have no way of knowing if the Reverend is who he says he is.

LUKE. *(Pacing up and down.)* We can't have strangers wandering in and out of this house. My instructions were to keep everybody out except the Chagos Island Government Representative.

DANIEL. Well the Reverend is here now, and he's gone to get his secretary, so there's going to be two more people, and there's not much we can do about it.

LUKE. *(Moves up to the R. window and looks out.)* I shall be watching them like a hawk. If he's not who he says he is, then I shall apply the interrogation technique specified in field agent's manual section 49, subsection 3C.

(He comes D. behind the couch.)

MARGARET. How do you remember all those sections and subsections. I could never do that.

LUKE. Ah, but you don't have my brain.

DANIEL. We know, and whoever has it should return it.

MARGARET. By the way Luke, you're no longer who you say you are.

LUKE. What do you mean?

MARGARET. You're not from the CIA-CIA. You're from the Culinary Institute of America.

LUKE. I am?

MARGARET. Yes, you're a chef.

LUKE. Why?

MARGARET. I made a mistake and Daniel covered. We couldn't let the Reverend know who you really are, could we?

LUKE. That's right, good thinking, I'm under cover now, a chef. I can do that.

MARGARET. And you have narcolepsy.

LUKE. Oh ... OK. Good. I can do fits.

DANIEL. Not epilepsy you idiot, narcolepsy. *(LUKE looks blank.)* You know, falling asleep all the time.

LUKE. Oh ... OK. Good. I can do that. *(Falls asleep.)*

DANIEL. *(Gets up and moves to LUKE, then whispers in his ear.)* What are you doing?

LUKE. *(Eyes still closed.)* I'm practicing.

DANIEL. Practice later! For heaven's sake, get outside and follow the preacher man!

LUKE. Right. I can do that.

(LUKE exits front door on the dead run leaving it wide open. DANIEL goes to close the front door as MARGARET starts to put coffee mugs, etc. on the tray.)

DANIEL. It makes you wonder where they find these agents and how they manage to train such idiots. *(Comes D. and picks up the tray.)* Here let me get that. He'd never have made it in the Marine Corps. The drill sergeants would have had him for breakfast.

(DANIEL exits to the kitchen. MARGARET watches him go, stands, picks up her purse and briefcase from behind the couch.)

MARGARET. You're one handsome hunk Mr. Warren, and I'm not finished with you yet. One way or another, before this night is over, your boots will be under my bed.

(MARGARET exits to bedroom 3, leaving the door open.)

DANIEL. *(Entering from the kitchen)* We've really got to tighten security around here if this meeting is to take place. Ms. Johnson, how do you propose we do it?

(MARGARET, who is in the bedroom, hears her name and comes to the door, but has only heard the last part of DANIEL's speech.)

MARGARET. Do it?

DANIEL. *(Comes down behind the couch.)* Yes, we both know what needs to be done.

MARGARET. We do?

DANIEL. Absolutely, I think we've been here long enough and we need to get down to business.

MARGARET. Sounds good to me.

DANIEL. *(Pacing a little.)* Right! First of all we need to find a way to do it without the preacher from hell finding out.

MARGARET. Way to go big boy!

DANIEL. *(Looking thoughtful he wanders D. to the drinks table.)* Timing may be tricky, but I think we can handle it.

MARGARET. Oooh, I'm so glad you think timing is important.

DANIEL. Right. The place should be private. Your room would be best.

MARGARET. Now you're talking!

DANIEL. O.K., now here's the plan. We shouldn't rush into this. We should create the right mood. It should proceed slowly in a relaxed atmosphere. Perhaps a glass or two of wine would help.

MARGARET. I must be better than I thought.

DANIEL. *(Turns and heads back U.S.)* And then, when the moment arrives we'll be in a position to take advantage of the situation. What do you think?

(He is now behind the couch, facing L. towards MARGARET. She hurls herself at him, and falls on top of him over the back of the couch, his legs in the air outspread.)

MARGARET. I love it! I love it! I love it! *(Kisses him passionately.)*

(Enter SAMUEL through the front door. He puts his umbrella in the umbrella stand. He is followed by MILLICENT, who is carrying two suitcases, which she puts down by the front door. MILLICENT, age 25-35, is Samuel's secretary. She is dressed in a long black raincoat over a dark brown, ankle length dress, with long sleeves. Her shoes look like work boots. She is the most unglamorous figure imaginable. She wears no makeup or jewelry. Her hair is tied up in a bun and she wears a pair of oversize glasses. She closes the door.)

SAMUEL. *(Sees DANIEL and MARGARET on the couch. He raises his hands to the heavens.)* I leave you for five minutes and sexual depravity rears its ugly head again. Millicent, hide your eyes. Ms. Johnson and Mr. Warren, I beseech you, do not let this innocent creature witness your lust and desire.

(DANIEL and MARGARET stand up and straighten out their clothing.)

SAMUEL. Millicent, this is Margaret Johnson and Daniel

Warren.

    MILLICENT. Hello.

    DANIEL. Here, please, let me have your coats.

(MILLICENT takes her coat off, but SAMUEL just stands there waiting for it to be removed from his shoulders.)

    MILLICENT. Thank you for helping us. It's really bad out there.

    MARGARET. You're welcome. Please, sit down.

(MARGARET sits in L. chair.)

    MILLICENT. Thank you.

(SAMUEL sits on the L. of the couch, MILLICENT sits on the R. of the couch.)

    MARGARET. You look chilled.

    DANIEL. Could I get you some coffee, or perhaps a glass of brandy?

    MILLICENT. Oh no, Samuel *(She looks at him with adoring eyes.)* has warned me about the evils of liquor.

    SAMUEL. That's right my dear, but you've been through a lot tonight. I think a small drop of brandy for medicinal purposes would be acceptable for both of us.

    DANIEL. Right.

(He goes D.R. to the drinks table.)

    SAMUEL. Any luck with the cell phone?

MARGARET. No, I'm sorry, it's still not working.

SAMUEL. Oh dear, Ms. Johnson, could you possibly accommodate two more weary souls overnight?

MARGARET. Well, Daniel?

DANIEL *(Indicates bedroom 1.)* Well, the chef has that room, and that only leaves this one other room *(Indicates bedroom 2)* besides my quarters at the rear.

SAMUEL. I see. Of course, I will need a room of my own, and as you and Mr. Warren will most certainly not be sharing a room, do you suppose you could share with Millicent?

MARGARET. I guess that's all right. Is that O.K. with you Millicent?

MILLICENT. That will be fine, thank you.

(DANIEL crosses L. behind the couch with a glass of brandy in each hand, which he then hands to SAMUEL and MILLICENT.)

DANIEL. Here you go.

MILLICENT. Samuel, are you sure this is all right?

(SAMUEL nods. MILLICENT takes a sip, coughs and then giggles.

There is a yell and a thud from outside followed by knocking on the window. Everyone watches as DANIEL goes up to the R. window, opens the drapes and slides open the window. We see LUKE hanging upside down, dripping wet.)

DANIEL. Hello.

LUKE. Hello.

DANIEL. What are you doing?

LUKE. What does it look like I'm doing?

DANIEL. Trying to get some blood to your brain?

MILLICENT. Who's that?

SAMUEL. Why is your chef hanging upside down outside the window?

MILLICENT. Maybe he's working on a recipe for pineapple upside down cake.

SAMUEL. Outside, in the rain?

MARGARET. Well,—er—it keeps him awake. *(MILLICENT giggles and sips her brandy.)* Let's face it. He has hang-ups.

SAMUEL. You have a narcoleptic chef, hanging by his feet, outside your window in the rain working on a recipe for pineapple upside down cake?

MARGARET. Yes, doesn't everybody?

LUKE. *(Yelling.)* Excuse me, if it's not too much trouble, and you can find the time to stop making jokes at my unfortunate predicament, I would appreciate it if someone would please come out and cut me down.

DANIEL. Hang in there Luke. *(Closes the window and the drapes.)* I'll get him down.

(He takes an umbrella and exits front door.)

MILLICENT. Oh Samuel, I like this. *(Takes another sip of brandy.)*

SAMUEL. Perhaps I should finish it for you.

(He reaches for her glass.)

MILLICENT. No! *(She clutches the glass tightly to her.)* I

mean, I'm still a bit chilled. *(Takes another sip and giggles.)*

MARGARET. Can I get you a drop more, Reverend?

SAMUEL. No thank you, I'm fine. I must keep a clear head.

MARGARET. And you, Millicent?

MILLICENT. I don't think I should. Samuel often preaches about how people can be corrupted by what he calls, "The Devil's Brew."

SAMUEL. I wouldn't put it in words exactly like that.

MILLICENT. You always put it in words exactly like that.

(Enter DANIEL and LUKE through the front door. DANIEL puts his umbrella in the stand and assists LUKE, who is totally soaked, and unsteady on his feet.)

DANIEL. Come on, you can change in my room.

(They both exit to the kitchen.)

MARGARET. So what brought you to this area?

MILLICENT. We were on our way to a revival where Samuel was scheduled to preach, but we got lost.

SAMUEL. Millicent, the Lord works in mysterious ways. I do not believe we were ever lost. I believe the Lord has a mission for me here.

(Enter DANIEL from the kitchen. He comes D.R. to the drinks table and pours himself a drink.)

MILLICENT. Is the chef all right?

DANIEL. Mr. James is a little shaken up, but he'll be fine.

MILLICENT. I'd like to meet him when he's back to normal.

DANIEL. I'm not sure the words normal and Luke James have ever been used in the same sentence before. He's just changing; he'll be out in a minute or two.

SAMUEL. Now Mr. Warren I still have no satisfactory explanation as to why your chef was hanging upside down outside the window in a blinding rainstorm.

MILLICENT. Maybe he just likes to hang out. *(Giggles.)*

SAMUEL. *(Glares at MILLICENT.)* Mr. Warren, what is going on?

(DANIEL crosses L. behind couch to MARGARET.)

DANIEL. Oh, nothing's going on, there's really a very simple explanation.

MARGARET. There is?

DANIEL. Of course.

MARGARET. I can't wait to hear this.

DANIEL. Ah, well—er—you see—er—you tell him Margaret.

MARGARET. Me?

DANIEL. Yes, you. Please explain to the Reverend about Luke.

MARGARET. *(Aside to DANIEL.)* You owe me for this one. *(Turns to SAMUEL.)* You see Reverend, the truth is, one of the extreme treatments for narcolepsy is to cool the body down while hanging upside down. This allows fresh blood to quickly flow into the brain, which stimulates the neurons in the part of the brain that tell him to sleep. This in turn keeps him awake.

SAMUEL. Amazing.

DANIEL. She is.… I mean it is, isn't it.

MILLICENT. It must be difficult having narcolepsy, if you

never know when you'll fall asleep, how would you know when to set the alarm?

(There is a series of bangs, crashes and yells off stage from LUKE.)

DANIEL. Now what?
MARGARET. *(Leaps to her feet.)* Take a break, I'll go.

(She exits to kitchen.)

DANIEL. *(Turns to MILLICENT.)* Can I get you another one?
MILLICENT. *(Stands, hands her glass to DANIEL who then crosses to the drinks table.)* Thank you.
SAMUEL. Millicent? Everything in moderation!
MILLICENT. Oh … just a small one then.

(MILLICENT sits while SAMUEL frowns disapprovingly.)

SAMUEL. I appreciate your hospitality Mr. Warren, but please remember that Millicent is an innocent, and we must be careful not to lead her astray. As you know alcohol is the root of all evil.
DANIEL. I thought it was money.
SAMUEL. Money is only evil when it is not used to do the Lord's work.
MILLICENT. And Samuel is always telling everybody how he needs money for the Lord's work.

(Enter MARGARET through the kitchen door, shaking her head

in disbelief. She comes D. R.)

MILLICENT. Is there a problem?
MARGARET. Just a slight accident.
DANIEL. What is it this time?
MARGARET. It seems Mr. James had this brilliant idea of standing with his back to the oven to dry his clothes, and they caught on fire. He then appears to have sprayed the entire kitchen and most of himself with a fire extinguisher, and I don't even want to guess how he got involved with all that ketchup.

(She sits R. chair.
There is a long agonized groan from the kitchen. They all look at the kitchen door as LUKE slowly appears. He is covered with white foam and has red streaks running down from his head.)

MILLICENT. *(Stands, moves U. to LUKE.)* Oh you look absolutely delicious. *(There is a stunned silence.)* Well, I mean you look just like a strawberry sundae.
DANIEL. Oh for heavens sakes, come on, let's get you cleaned up … again!

(DANIEL hands MILLICENT her drink and heads U. They go to the kitchen and as LUKE turns, we see that the rear of his pants have a large burned hole exposing boxers with hearts all over them.)

SAMUEL. Hide your eyes, Millicent.

(MILLICENT covers her eyes, but we see her peeking.)

MILLICENT. I thought you were suppose to wear your heart on your sleeve, I never heard about wearing your heart on your—

SAMUEL. Millicent, you must forget what you just saw. The Lord requires us to remain pure, both in mind and body.

MILLICENT. But Samuel, why would he have hearts on his shorts?

SAMUEL. I really don't think it's appropriate for us to be discussing Mr. James' underwear.

MILLICENT. Well, alright, but hearts?

MARGARET. Ahem— *(Stands.)* Millicent, perhaps you'd like to change into some dry clothes, let me get your suitcase and I'll show you our room.

(She gets Millicent's suitcase, carries it to the door of bedroom 3, and opens the door.)

MILLICENT. *(Stands.)* Thank you, that would be nice.

(She downs the rest of the brandy in one gulp, puts the glass on the coffee table and moves to the door of bedroom 3.)

MARGARET. I'm afraid there's only the one bathroom in this part of the cabin, but there's a nice size closet where you can put your things. Would you excuse us for a moment Reverend?

(MILLICENT exits to bedroom 3, followed by MARGARET carrying the suitcase.)

SAMUEL. Of course.

(SAMUEL watches them go, looks around a little furtively, then

moves quickly R. to the drinks table, pours himself a shot of brandy, downs it in one gulp, and quickly returns to the L. of the couch.
MARGARET enters from bedroom 3.)

MARGARET. Reverend, let me show you to your room.

(She crosses R. and opens the door of bedroom 2.)

SAMUEL. Thank you. *(Goes up and gets his suitcase.)* I have some important papers in my suitcase, which I need to study.

MARGARET. You should be very comfortable in here.

SAMUEL. Thank you, however, my mission is not one of comfort, Ms. Johnson. *(He enters the bedroom and as MARGARET walks slowly L. SAMUEL reappears in the doorway.)* Incidentally, I have some special dietary requirements, which I would like to discuss with you later, when the cook is awake.

(He exits to bedroom 2 and closes the door.)

MARGARET. *(Stands for a moment with her mouth wide open. Runs to the kitchen and calls out.)* Mr. Warren, Mr. James.

(DANIEL enters immediately.)

DANIEL. What is it?
MARGARET. *(Moves D.L.)* It's him, the preacher, it's him.
DANIEL. *(Moves R. behind couch)* What?
MARGARET. The Reverend Samuel Abernathy is the Chagos Islands' representative.

DANIEL. What?

MARGARET. He just gave me the code word.

DANIEL. Are you sure?

MARGARET. It has to be him. How else would he know the code word?

DANIEL. It makes no sense. Why would he disguise himself as a preacher?

MARGARET. Well, it is a known fact that many religious leaders in small island nations hold important government positions.

DANIEL. I didn't know that. But if he really is who he says he is, why didn't he just say the code word right away?

MARGARET. How would he have known who I am? He thinks you and I are just here for a weekend together. He doesn't know I work for the State Department. Come to think of it, how would he know now?

DANIEL. *(Sits couch R.)* That's a good point, but, with the phones down, we have no way to confirm any of this. Perhaps Millicent is the answer. Maybe we can find out by having Luke interview her. If she really is a government secretary, even the genius from the Central Idiots Academy ought to be able to handle that. In the mean time, just don't do anything.

MARGARET. Well, I could do one thing.

DANIEL. What's that?

MARGARET. *(Lunges for him on the couch, but misses as DANIEL stands up)* Plant one on you big boy.

DANIEL. *(Breaks away.)* Ms. Johnson, please, what are you doing?

MARGARET. Obviously not basking in the warmth of your welcome.

DANIEL. Ms. Johnson, can't we just be friends?

MARGARET. I don't know. I've never had a friend before.

DANIEL. I'm sure you have lots of friends.

MARGARET. No, no. I mean I've never "*HAD*" a friend before.

DANIEL. Really Ms. Johnson, you're incorrigible, I give up. *(MARGARET stands and moves towards DANIEL.)* Let me re-phrase that. I'd better get Luke out here as fast as I can. In the meantime don't give anything away to the Reverend.

(DANIEL exits to kitchen.)

MARGARET. *(Almost to herself.)* Don't worry, the only one I'll be giving anything away to is you, my gentleman girene.

(There is a loud knocking on the front door. MARGARET opens the door to reveal HEATHER ANN FARADAY.

She steps hurriedly into the room to get out of the rain. Age 30-35, she is smart, calculating, beautiful, and very sensuous, but as we shall see, is not what she appears to be. She is, in fact, DANIEL's partner, employed by OPEC. She is wearing a pastel raincoat and matching hat, a pair of blue jeans, a cashmere sweater and fashionable ankle boots. She carries a small overnight case. We see that the bottoms of her jeans are soaking wet.)

HEATHER. *(Taking off her hat and coat.)* Oh, hello, is Mr. Cole here?

MARGARET. I'm afraid not.

HEATHER. Oh dear.

MARGARET. I'm Margaret Johnson. Can I help you?

HEATHER. I don't know? Who are you?

MARGARET. Well, I'm—er—er—a friend of Mr. Cole and I had arranged with him to use his house for a little business meeting. Who are you?

HEATHER. I'm Heather Ann Faraday. I was hoping Mr. Cole would be here. You see I live just the other side of the creek and my power went out in the storm. I saw the lights on and I was hoping I could stay here for the night.

MARGARET. I see. Why don't you give me your coat. *(Takes Heather's hat and coat and hangs them on the coat rack.)* Please, sit down.

HEATHER. Thank you.

(She sits on the L. side of the couch and tries unsuccessfully to take off her boots.)

MARGARET. *(Sits on R. chair.)* So, you know Mr. Cole then?

HEATHER. Of course, we've been neighbors ever since I got divorced and moved into my cabin three years ago. We even cook for each other once in awhile. I'm surprised he's not here, I just saw him yesterday.

MARGARET. I don't want to alarm you, but Mr. Cole had to go for some medical tests earlier today, and we don't expect him back tonight.

HEATHER. Really, he never said anything to me.

MARGARET. *(Stands.)* Would you excuse me for a moment, I need to let Mr. Warren know you are here.

HEATHER Who's Mr. Warren?

MARGARET. He's—er—er an associate of mine.

HEATHER. May I use the bathroom to dry off a little?

MARGARET. Of course, that's the door there. *(Points to the bathroom.)* Excuse me.

*(MARGARET exits to the kitchen. HEATHER exits to the bath-
room.*
*Enter SAMUEL from bedroom 2, he looks around to see if any-
one is there, heads D.R. to the drinks table and facing R.
pours himself a drink.*
*Enter MILLICENT from bedroom 3. She stands and watches him
gulp his drink. She covers her face with her hands in disbelief, rushes back into the bedroom, and closes the door.*
*SAMUEL, still at the drinks table, with his glass in hand, is
about to pour another drink, when HEATHER enters from
the bathroom and comes D. Startled, SAMUEL quickly puts
the glass down and moves UL behind the R. chair.)*

HEATHER. Oh, I'm sorry, did I startle you?

SAMUEL. Oh no, indeed no, I just didn't realize there was
anyone else here. Where are my manners, allow me to introduce
myself. I am the Reverend Samuel Abernathy.

HEATHER. How do you do, I'm Heather Ann Faraday.

(They shake hands.)

SAMUEL. Would you care to sit down?

*(HEATHER moves to the couch L. end, SAMUEL sits in the chair
R.)*

HEATHER. Are you a friend of Mr. Cole?
SAMUEL. Who?
HEATHER. Mr. Cole, he owns this house.

SAMUEL. I'm afraid I've never met Mr. Cole. My car broke down earlier this evening in the storm and my secretary and I took shelter here. The Lord works in wondrous ways. It seems He summoned me here, and I arrived just in time to intervene in an immoral situation of the utmost depravity.

HEATHER. What?

SAMUEL. I mean, those two misguided souls who were about to embark on an illicit liaison.

HEATHER. Which two misguided souls?

SAMUEL. Ms. Johnson and Mr. Warren.

HEATHER. *(Frowning.)* Mr. Warren?

SAMUEL. Oh yes, indeed.

HEATHER. Really? Ms. Johnson just told me she arranged to use the cabin for business, and that Mr. Warren was her associate.

(She is still trying to remove one of her boots.)

SAMUEL. The only business those two are conducting is monkey business.

HEATHER. Oh. *(She pauses.)* Ooh! I see.

SAMUEL. I hope you never do.

HEATHER. You know, I'm really embarrassed to even ask, but I desperately want to get out of these wet boots, and I can't seem to get them off. Would it offend you if I asked for your help?

SAMUEL. Not at all, I am here to be of service. *(He stands in front of her facing U.S. and tugs at the L. boot. She starts to slide off the couch, while nothing happens with the boot.)* Goodness me, it doesn't seem to be coming off.

HEATHER. Here, try this; let me brace myself with my

other foot.

(She now turns on the couch and braces her R. foot on the R. end of the couch. SAMUEL moves to the R. side of the couch and begins to pull on her L. boot. There is some tugging, but to no avail.)

SAMUEL. Here, let me try it this way.

(He now turns around facing R. with his back to HEATHER and places her left leg between his, holding the boot with his hands. As he tugs on the boot HEATHER moves her left leg and catches him in the crotch. He stands bolt upright, eyes bulging and yells.)

SAMUEL. AAIIEEGH!!
HEATHER. Oops! Sorry. *(Grins.)*
SAMUEL. *(In a high voice.)* That's quite *(He pauses then continues in a normal voice)* alright.
SAMUEL. Let's give it one more try.

(He turns around again and tackles the problem from the front. Eventually, with one giant pull, HEATHER falls backward on the couch as SAMUEL falls on top of her between her legs.
MILLICENT enters from bedroom 3 and sees SAMUEL and HEATHER. With a cry of anguish, she goes back into the bedroom and closes the door, as DANIEL enters from the kitchen, and comes D. behind the couch.)

DANIEL. Well, barbie my behind and call me a brisket,

what have we got here? *(Arms outspread and palms up.)* Witness the sins of the flesh.

SAMUEL. *(Stands as HEATHER sits up.)* I can assure you Mr. Warren it is not what it appears to be.

DANIEL. Well, you could have fooled me. I leave you for five minutes and sexual depravity rears it's ugly head.

(He raises his hands, mimicking SAMUEL.)

SAMUEL. Really, this is too much.

DANIEL. *(Laughing.)* I want you to know I cannot condone this lascivious behavior.

SAMUEL. This is intolerable. How dare you mock a man of the cloth. I will not stand here and listen to any more of this. Excuse me, Ms. Faraday.

(SAMUEL exits to bedroom 2.)

HEATHER. It really was an accident, we simply fell over.

DANIEL. *(Sits R. chair.)* I'm sure it was. But it's such fun to tease him.

(MILLICENT enters from bedroom 3.)

MILLICENT. Oh, I'm sorry, I hope I'm not disturbing you. I wanted to talk to Samuel.

DANIEL. I'm afraid he just left. Millicent, may I introduce you to Ms. Faraday.

HEATHER. Hello, please, call me Heather.

MILLICENT. Hi, do you live here?

HEATHER. Oh no, I live across the creek. My power went

out in the storm. Since I know Mr. Cole, who owns this cabin, I came over here to see if he could put me up for the night.

MILLICENT. Oh, you poor dear, you're really wet, maybe a brandy would help. I can recommend it.

HEATHER. Maybe later, right now I would love to get out of these wet boots. Mr. Warren, perhaps you could give me a hand?

DANIEL. Please, call me Daniel. Sure, why don't we give it a try. *(He tugs and one boot comes off.)* Here we go. *(The other boot comes off.)*

HEATHER. Thank you so much.

DANIEL. Your jeans are soaked. Do you have anything to change into?

HEATHER. No, I'm afraid not.

MILLICENT. Maybe I can help. I'm afraid I don't have any jeans, but I do have a skirt if that would help, and let's see if I have a pair of shoes that would fit.

HEATHER. Oh, I brought some shoes, but a skirt would be nice. Thank you.

MILLICENT. Why don't you come with me?

(HEATHER picks up the boots and her suitcase then follows MILLICENT. They exit to bedroom 3.
Enter LUKE from the kitchen, now all cleaned up, and wearing a reasonable facsimile of a chef's outfit.)

LUKE: *(Comes L. behind the couch.)* Well, what do you think?

DANIEL. *(Moves U. to LUKE.)* Listen, there's another woman here.

LUKE. Another woman? Who?

DANIEL. Heather Faraday. She says she's a neighbor and knows Mr. Cole. Her power went out, and now she has to stay the night.

LUKE. This isn't a safe house, it's a bed and breakfast. Did you check her ID?

DANIEL. Isn't that supposed to be your job?

LUKE. Yes. Right, I can do that.

DANIEL. First things first, Millicent will be out in a minute. We need to find out if she and the Reverend really are representing the Chagos Islands' Government. Can you do that and remain incognito?

LUKE. *(Pauses.)* I thought we were in Virginia.

DANIEL. I mean in a subtle way, without revealing you're an agent.

LUKE. Subtle is my middle name.

DANIEL. You're about as subtle as a sledgehammer. Just remember, you're a chef.

LUKE. That's the only thing that worries me a little. I don't know anything about food. What do I do if they ask me questions about cooking and stuff?

DANIEL. Well, be kind of vague, and you are a narcoleptic, so you could always fall asleep if you really get stuck.

LUKE. Right. I can do that.

(MILLICENT enters from bedroom 3.)

MILLICENT. I found a skirt. Heather's changing. *(Sees LUKE.)* Oh, hello, you must be the chef.

DANIEL. Millicent, I'd like to introduce you to Luke James.

LUKE. Hello.

MILLICENT. Hi. You look a little different from the last

time I saw you. Are you alright?

DANIEL. He's never been alright.

LUKE. I just had a slight accident, but I'm fine, thank you.

DANIEL. Right, I'll leave you two to get acquainted; I'll be in my room if you need me.

(DANIEL exits to kitchen.
They sit on the couch. MILLICENT L., LUKE R.)

MILLICENT. I am so excited to meet a real chef. My hobby is cooking and I watch all the TV shows. I have a million questions I'd love to ask you.

LUKE. Oh dear.

MILLICENT. I'm sorry. Was that rude?

LUKE. No, that's fine. However, before we get to that, I'm fascinated by the Reverend Abernathy's line of work. Tell me, do you always travel with him?

MILLICENT. Yes, most of the time.

LUKE. What exactly do you do?

MILLICENT. Well, my main job is to keep track of the finances. In the past few years, considerable sums of money have been required.

LUKE. Really?

MILLICENT. Yes, particularly in the area of social services. The Reverend is especially keen on supporting programs for the needy.

LUKE. I see, and he alone handles all the negotiations for those funds?

MILLICENT. I wouldn't really call them negotiations. He feels that he is in such a position of strength, that he always gets what he needs.

LUKE. But the decisions are his to make?

MILLICENT. Definitely, but he is responsible to a higher authority.

LUKE. Of course.

MILLICENT. If you don't mind, can you tell me what it's like to be a chef?

LUKE. It's—er—er—different.

MILLICENT. Different?

LUKE. Well,—er—every day you cook something different, right?

MILLICENT. I guess you do. What's your favorite dish?

LUKE. A plate.

MILLICENT. What?

LUKE. A plate of—er—er—

(He stares straight ahead for a brief moment, then very suddenly and deliberately his chin falls, his head turns sideways a little, his eyes close and he falls asleep.)

MILLICENT. Mr. James? Mr. James? Oh dear.

(She waves her hand in front of his face, looks around, then goes to the drinks table and pours herself a drink, which she gulps down, then returns to her seat on the couch.)

LUKE. *(Wakes up.)* Oh dear, did I fall asleep?

MILLICENT. Yes, I think you did. Would you like a brandy? It seems to help me.

LUKE. I'm not sure I should, being on duty and all.

MILLICENT. Duty?

LUKE. Er—cooking duty, I have to cook tonight, but I suppose one couldn't hurt.

MILLICENT. Of course not.

(LUKE moves to the drinks table.)

LUKE. *(Pours a drink.)* Would you like one too?

MILLICENT. Oh no, Samuel says, *(Mimics SAMUEL.)* "Everything in moderation."

LUKE. May I ask how long you've known the Reverend?

MILLICENT. Yes.

(There is a long pause.)

LUKE. Well, are you going to tell me?

MILLICENT. Tell you what?

LUKE. How long you've known the Reverend?

MILLICENT. Would you like me to?

LUKE. Yes.

MILLICENT. Alright.

(Another pause.)

LUKE. Are you going to answer my question?

MILLICENT. What question?

LUKE. *(To himself.)* And I thought cooking was hard.

MILLICENT. You think cooking is hard?

LUKE. Yes,—er—I mean no. What about my question?

MILLICENT. I don't know...

LUKE. You don't know how long you've known the Reverend?

MILLICENT. Of course I do. I've known him for two years.

LUKE. *(Turns towards MILLICENT.)* Ah ha! So you don't really know him that well.

MILLICENT. Well, I thought I did, but I'm just beginning to realize that perhaps he's not everything he claims to be.

LUKE. What?

MILLICENT. It doesn't matter. I've been dying to ask you how do you stop a soufflé from going flat? *(LUKE still at the drinks table stares straight ahead then repeats the falling asleep routine, MILLICENT moves R. to the drinks table, waves her hand in front of his face, there is no reaction, so she takes the drink out of his hand and gulps it down, then returns the empty glass to his hand.)* Was it something I said? *(There is no reaction from Luke.)* Mr. James?

LUKE. *(Wakes up.)* What?

MILLICENT. Oh dear, you fell asleep again.

LUKE. Oh, I'm sorry.

(He gives the empty glass a puzzled look.)

MILLICENT. That's O.K., I know you can't help it.

LUKE. You do?

MILLICENT. Of course, I know you suffer from narcolepsy, Samuel told me. It must be very difficult.

LUKE. You really have a heart of gold, don't you?

MILLICENT. *(Giggles.)* And I remember your hearts. *(Now embarrassed.)* Oh, that's very naughty. I—er—er—really ought to check on Ms. Faraday. Maybe the skirt won't fit. Um … excuse me.

(She moves in a great hurry to bedroom 3 and exits, closing the

*door. LUKE, also embarrassed, turns away R. and puts his
glass on the bar, then sits on couch C.
Enter from the kitchen DANIEL, followed closely by MARGARET
reaching for his derriere.)*

DANIEL. Oh-ooh, ma'am, I've told you before— *(Stops as
he sees LUKE.)* Oh, there you are. So how did the interview go?

(He comes D. and sits in the L. chair.)

MARGARET. Well, what did you find out? *(Comes D. and
sits in the R. chair.)* Is he the representative?
LUKE. *(Pauses and looks around the room, then indicates to
them that they should lean closer.)* From my interrogation of said
subject, and applying all the techniques at my disposal, while
using subtle maneuvers to persuade the said subject to disclose
certain information, I have determined that the Reverend MAY
be the representative.

(DANIEL and MARGARET look at each other, then at LUKE.)

DANIEL & MARGARET. *(Together.)* MAY be?
LUKE. Yes.
DANIEL. Alright, tell us exactly what you found out.
LUKE. Well, he alone handles all the negotiations.

(There is a long pause.)

MARGARET. That's it?
LUKE. There's more. *(He indicates that they should join him
on the couch. DANIEL and MARGARET look at each other, then*

move to the arms of the couch.) He is always in such a position of
strength that he never really needs to negotiate.

MARGARET. Oh, dear, that could be trouble.

DANIEL. What else?

LUKE. *(Looks around the room again, and now indicates
that they should sit next to him on the couch. They do.)* He is responsible to a higher authority.

DANIEL. Well we know that.

(MARGARET and DANIEL return to their chairs.)

MARGARET. So, the bottom line is we still don't know for
sure. We need to create the opportunity for me to be alone with
him so we can confirm it one way or another. It's not really the
ideal situation with all these people here, but it's all we've got.

LUKE. I know, why don't I—

DANIEL. No.

LUKE. No?

DANIEL. No.

LUKE. But ….

DANIEL. No

MARGARET. Maybe you can help Luke. Do you think you
can you keep Millicent busy in the kitchen?

LUKE. *(Stands.)* I can do that.

MARGARET. Daniel, can you keep Heather busy? But not
too busy, if you know what I mean.

DANIEL. Sure, it sounds like it's let up a little. I'll suggest
we go check out her cabin.

(He moves U. to window and looks out.
Enter MILLICENT and HEATHER from bedroom 3. HEATHER

is now wearing a dark skirt and flat shoes.)

MILLICENT. I hope we're not disturbing you?

MARGARET. Oh no, we were just going over the dinner plans for this evening, and the chef wondered if perhaps you'd like to help him? Isn't that right Luke?

LUKE. Oh, yes.

MILLICENT. I'd love to. I've always wanted to work with a real chef.

(MILLICENT hooks her arm in LUKE's and they exit to the kitchen.)

HEATHER. Is he safe in a kitchen?

MARGARET. Oh, he'll be fine.

DANIEL. He can function quite well when the moon is full and the wind is in the right direction. *(Turns to HEATHER.)* It's just about stopped raining. Perhaps this is a chance for us to go and take a look at your generator.

HEATHER. What a good idea.

DANIEL. Right, I'll just get my raincoat and a flashlight. I'll be right back.

(DANIEL exits to kitchen.
HEATHER moves U. to the coat rack and puts on her raincoat and hat.)

HEATHER. I'm not sure if we'll make it across the creek, the bridge is very low.

MARGARET. You're a lucky lady. You have a strong, good-looking ex-marine with you. I'm sure if there's a way he'll find it. I just hope it's only the generator he checks out.

HEATHER. Oh, he's not my type.

MARGARET. Well, he's certainly mine.

HEATHER. What makes you say that?

MARGARET. He's single.

(Enter DANIEL from the kitchen wearing a raincoat and carrying a flashlight.)

DANIEL. *(Now at the front door.)* All set, let's go.

(He opens the door for HEATHER, and then follows her out, closing the door.
MARGARET looks around, moves R. and knocks on Samuel's door. SAMUEL opens the door.)

MARGARET. Excuse me, Reverend, but I was wondering if I might have a word with you.

SAMUEL. Certainly.

MARGARET. *(Moves L. a little.)* First, I would like to apologize for Mr. Warren's remarks earlier. I'm sure that he didn't mean anything by them.

SAMUEL. It is the very nature of man to belittle that which he does not understand. He is already forgiven, for the Lord says, "Do not judge, and you will not be judged. Do not condemn, and you will not be condemned. Forgive, and you will be forgiven."

(MARGARET sits on the couch as SAMUEL sits in the R. chair.)

MARGARET. That is very generous of you. Now that we both know *(She pauses and leans forward.)* the cook is awake, perhaps we can get down to business.

SAMUEL. Certainly.

MARGARET. I do understand how delicate the situation is, but I want to assure you that we will do everything in our power to accommodate your needs.

SAMUEL. Thank you, that's very kind of you.

MARGARET. Now, perhaps you could explain to me, what is your primary concern?

SAMUEL. It's oil, madam.

MARGARET. Well of course, it's everyone's concern.

SAMUEL. What I'm referring to is thousand island oil.

MARGARET. Are there really a thousand islands?

SAMUEL. What?

MARGARET. The Chagos Islands, are there really a thousand of them?

SAMUEL. What in heaven's name are you talking about?

MARGARET. What are you talking about?

SAMUEL. My dietary needs, I am allergic to certain kinds of oil, usually used in creamy salad dressings.

MARGARET. Then you're not a Chagosian?

SAMUEL. Certainly not, I'm a Presbyterian.

(The front door bursts open and DANIEL rushes in.)

DANIEL. *(Running towards the kitchen.)* There's a fire in the kitchen.

(He exits to the kitchen.
MARGARET jumps to her feet and follows him off to the kitchen.)

MARGARET. Oh Lord, not again!

(Enter HEATHER from the front door. She closes it behind her and takes off her coat and hat and hangs them on the coat rack.
SAMUEL stands and moves UR.)

SAMUEL. What happened?
HEATHER. We were only about half way down to the creek, when we saw smoke pouring out of the kitchen window.
SAMUEL. Oh dear, I hope no one is hurt. Maybe I should render some assistance.
HEATHER. *(Sits on the couch L. side.)* I'm sure they have it under control.
SAMUEL. Ms. Faraday, I must apologize. I was quite embarrassed about the compromising situation in which Mr. Warren found us. He really doesn't seem to believe it was accidental.
HEATHER. That's ... oh dear!

(HEATHER starts to pat her lap and the couch, then drops to her knees in front of the couch.)

SAMUEL. What is it?
HEATHER. I seem to have lost a contact.
SAMUEL. Here, let me help.

(He gets down on his hands and knees and starts searching.)

HEATHER. Don't move, I think I see it.

(HEATHER reaches underneath him, then accidentally knocks one of his arms out. He collapses on top of her, as MILLI-CENT enters from the kitchen. She sees SAMUEL and

HEATHER, screams and rushes off into bedroom 3. Before HEATHER and SAMUEL can disentangle themselves, LUKE, hearing the scream, enters from the kitchen, his face and shirt are now black.)

LUKE. Millicent, Millicent, it's alright.

(He follows her into bedroom 3.
Enter immediately DANIEL and MARGARET from the kitchen.)

DANIEL. *(Moves behind the couch.)* Well, dunk me in decaf and call me a donut, what have we got here? *(Arms outspread and palms up.)* Witness the sins of the flesh. I leave you for five minutes and sexual depravity rears its ugly head again.

SAMUEL. Dear Lord, this is too much. *(Gets up and with what little dignity he can muster, prepares to storm off to his room.)* Once again Mr. Warren, you misinterpret what you see. You wrongly accuse me. How dare you pass judgment.

(SAMUEL exits to bedroom 2, and closes the door.)

DANIEL. I'd better go and clean up Luke's mess. Again.

(DANIEL exits to kitchen. HEATHER stands up and slowly turns to MARGARET who has now come DR.)

HEATHER. Hello Margaret Johnson from the State Department. Let me introduce myself. The cook is awake.

CURTAIN

ACT II

Scene 1

(Later the same evening.
As the curtain rises we see MARGARET on the couch L. side looking at papers with her open brief case on her lap. DANIEL is in front of the fireplace, leaning on the mantle. The drapes are open.)

DANIEL. Tell me, how are the negotiations going?

MARGARET. They're not. If anything they're moving backwards. That woman is impossible. Her demands are absolutely ridiculous. At a rough guess, I estimate she's asking for about 40 billion dollars, and that's just the first year.

DANIEL. Really?

MARGARET. You know demands like that are not usually made without benefit of a gun and a getaway car.

(She closes the brief case and puts it on the floor L. side of the couch.)

DANIEL. I'm surprised. She seemed very pleasant and easy-going at dinner, she even volunteered to stay in the kitchen and help Millicent with the dishes. Well, I guess you can't judge a book by its cover.

MARGARET. Unless it's that hunk on the cover of all those

romance novels. And speaking of hunks and covers, *(Stands and moves sexily towards him.)* I know of one hunk I'd like to see under my covers.

(DANIEL starts to back away. LUKE enters from the front door wearing the orange raincoat and carrying the FARTAD. He closes the front door as DANIEL and MARGARET turn to look at him.)

DANIEL. What's it doing?
LUKE. The storm is picking up again. Very heavy rain right now.

(MARGARET returns to the couch as DANIEL sits in the L. chair.)

MARGARET. What were you doing out there?

(LUKE hangs up his coat, puts down the FARTAD and comes D.)

LUKE. Well, since the phone still isn't working, and we know that Ms. Faraday is the Chagos Islands representative, I considered it strategically prudent, according to field agents manual section 4, sub section 2.3, to further address certain exterior restrictive devices around the perimeter of said property, and replace them with concealed multiple audible warning devices.

(He sits on R. chair.)

DANIEL & MARGARET. What?
LUKE. Replace the booby traps with noisemakers. And in

addition, I have hotwired the window frames.

DANIEL & MARGARET. *(Together.)* What?

LUKE. Using a thousand watt converter from my FARTAD, in accordance with security manual section 45, sub section 7, paragraph 13, anyone touching the window will be immediately subjected to very considerable voltage.

DANIEL. Idiot central strikes again.

LUKE. What's idiot central?

MARGARET. He doesn't get it does he?

DANIEL. I doubt he'd get it if it came in a large box marked "IT" in foot high neon letters.

MARGARET. *(Laughing.)* Incidentally Luke, we should congratulate you.

LUKE. No thanks are necessary, it's just part of my job.

MARGARET. What I'm congratulating you on is your cooking. The meal was actually quite good.

LUKE. Well, I have to confess, it was Millicent who prepared most of it. She really is very talented in the kitchen. I just pretended to supervise. By the way, where's the Reverend?

DANIEL. If you mean "The Parsimonious Preacher" who can't keep his hands to himself, he's in his room.

MARGARET. Aren't you being a little harsh?

DANIEL. Perhaps, but his favorite song has got to be "Reach Out and Touch Someone."

(LUKE leaps to his feet, puts his index finger to his lips as if to say 'sh.' He then forms a 'V' with his index and middle finger. He points his fingers towards his eyes and then towards the window, indicating he has seen something. He strikes a karate pose, charges upstage, trips over the FARTAD, and falls flat on his face. He gets up, smiles at MARGARET and

DANIEL, then flings open the front door and runs out with a horrendous karate type yell, "EEIYAAAH." There are tremendous metallic clanging, banging, and thumping noises as DANIEL rushes up to the front door and looks out, he then turns and smiles at MARAGARET as LUKE reappears with a metal bucket stuck on his head, and a string of tin cans wrapped around his body trailing behind him. [SEE AUTHOR'S NOTES.] He is helped in by RANGER DON.
RANGER DON is in fact DONNA, who is the Chagos Islands representative disguised as a man. She can be any age, and is dressed in a typical forest ranger uniform, including a hat or cap. She has on a rain poncho or slicker, and is wearing a fake mustache and glasses.)

RANGER DON. Excuse me, but does this belong to you?

(LUKE makes muffled noises from within the bucket.)

DANIEL. I'm afraid so. I'm very sorry. We don't normally let him out without a leash.

(DANIEL closes front door. LUKE continues to make louder noises from within the bucket. He tries unsuccessfully to remove it, and, in doing so, manages to become more entangled in the tin cans, making even more noise.
MILLICENT enters from the kitchen.)

MILLICENT. I heard this noise…ooh, *(Rushes up to Luke.)* you poor dear, sweet thing.

(She puts her arms around him, and tries to peer up underneath

the bucket.
Enter SAMUEL, who stops in the doorway of bedroom 2.)

SAMUEL. How am I supposed to commune with the Lord? There wasn't this much noise when the walls of Jericho were falling. *(Notices MILLICENT.)* Millicent, what do you think you are doing?

(MILLICENT takes LUKE's arm and moves towards the kitchen with him. Before they exit, she turns D.S., looks directly at SAMUEL for a moment, then with a roll of her eyes and a toss of her head, she turns abruptly and exits with LUKE.)

DANIEL. *(Turns to RANGER DON.)* Now sir, may I ask who you are, and what you're doing here?
RANGER DON. *(Opens the slicker to reveal a ranger badge.)* I'm Ranger Don. This is part of my territory. The storm has caused some power outages and some of the roads are impassable. I'm checking out all the cabins to see if anyone needs help.
DANIEL. I see, I didn't know that was part of a ranger's job.
RANGER DON. Normally it isn't, but all these cabins are actually on national park property.
MARGARET. I'm so sorry that you were disturbed, Reverend. Why don't you come and sit down. *(SAMUEL sits R. chair.)* And you too, Ranger Don. I was just about to get a little brandy, how about a small one just to warm you up. *(Crosses R. to the drinks table.)* Of course Reverend, I know you won't want one.

(SAMUEL's reaction makes it clear that he really would like one, but he just smiles politely at MARGARET.)

RANGER DON. *(Moves DL. to the fireplace.)* Well, maybe just a real quick one. I've got several other cabins to check on, and it looks like a long night.

DANIEL. Right, I'll just go see how bucket head is doing.

(DANIEL picks up the FARTAD and exits to the kitchen.)

SAMUEL. Ranger Don, my car broke down just down the road from here, when do you think a tow truck would be able to get here?

RANGER DON. Definitely not before tomorrow. And even that is doubtful. There are reports of rockslides and several trees are down. Only emergency vehicles are allowed in right now.

MARGARET. *(Moves L. and hands a drink to RANGER DON.)* Here you are.

(She takes her own drink and sits on the L. chair.)

RANGER DON. Thanks. *(Sips the brandy.)*

SAMUEL. I was just musing on how similar our vocations are. We both have the responsibility of rescuing lost souls, you, in the physical world, and I in the spiritual realm.

RANGER DON. I never really thought about it like that. However, my job is not in fact about rescuing people, as much as it is protecting the environment from their irresponsible behavior.

SAMUEL. There, you see, we are alike. I too must protect people from the attacks of Satan and their own irresponsible behavior. *(He gives MARGARET a "look.")* Don't I, Ms. Johnson?

MARGARET. I believe Ranger Don has more important things to do than sit here moralizing about other people's behavior, Reverend.

RANGER DON. *(Moving UC.)* You're right. I should be off. Thanks for the drink. I'll check back with you later. Goodnight for now.

(RANGER DON exits front door, closing it behind him.)

MARGARET. If you'll excuse me for just a moment or two Reverend, I'd better go and see how the bucket brigade is doing.

(She exits to the kitchen.
SAMUEL stands up and looks furtively around, then crosses R. to the drinks table, quickly pours himself a shot of brandy and downs it in one gulp. He hears voices coming from the kitchen and quickly returns to the chair.
Enter from the kitchen MARGARET, followed by MILLICENT assisting LUKE. LUKE is still wearing the bucket, but minus the tin cans.)

MARGARET. Of all the stupid, idiotic things, I can't believe he is still stuck in this bucket.

(MILLICENT guides LUKE to the couch and they both sit.)

MILLICENT. Well, at least we can try to make him comfortable while he's in this predicament.

(LUKE makes muffled noises from the bucket.)

MARGARET. *(Now behind the couch.)* Listen you guys, if it went on, it's got to come off. I've sent Daniel out to look for a crowbar.

MILLICENT. Oh no, please, not a crowbar.

(She looks up under the bucket, there is a moment's silence.)

SAMUEL. Is he alright?

MILLICENT. Yes, I think so, but he does look a little pale. *(Giggles.)* I think he's asleep. *(LUKE makes louder noises from within the bucket.)* Oops, sorry, I guess I'm wrong. Hang in there, Luke. Can I get you anything?

(LUKE shakes his head " no.")

SAMUEL. *(Stands.)* May I be of some assistance? Perhaps if we twist it.

(LUKE shakes his head frantically, with loud muffled " no's.")

MARGARET. That's probably a good idea Reverend. Millicent, could you sit on him please?

(MILLICENT stands.)

SAMUEL. No, no Millicent. *(He quickly intervenes and sits on Luke's lap instead, with his arms around him.)* Alright Ms. Johnson, give it a twist.

MILLICENT. Oh, please be careful.

(More muffled noises from under the bucket. MARGARET twists and the bucket comes off as DANIEL enters from the kitchen with a crowbar. He sees SAMUEL sitting on LUKE's lap,

with his arms around him.)

DANIEL. *(Moves down behind the couch.)* Well, sizzle my sit-upon and call me a sausage, what have we got here. You never cease to amaze me, Reverend.

(SAMUEL looks at DANIEL, looks at LUKE, and then realizes he is sitting on LUKE's lap with his arms around him. He jumps up and leaps backwards. MILLICENT sits, then cradles LUKE's head against her chest.)

SAMUEL. You don't think that I, that he, that we…. Oh, once again Mr. Warren, you condemn the innocent. Scripture says, "Judge not, lest you yourself be found wanting." I was simply trying to lend some assistance. I shall treat your insidious insinuation with the contempt it so justly deserves. Once again, Madam, *(He gives MARGARET a slight bow.)*, Millicent, good evening.

(He exits to bedroom 2.)

MARGARET. *(Laughing.)* You're really bad, you know that?
DANIEL. I know, but he's just such a pompous….
MILLICENT. Please Mr. Warren, I'm beginning to realize he may not be perfect, but can we at least, not make fun of him?
DANIEL. You're right Millicent. I apologize.
MILLICENT. *(To LUKE.)* Oh you poor thing, are you feeling alright?
LUKE. *(Still has his head against MILLICENT.)* I've got a little ringing in my ears, but I'm sure I'll be back to normal soon.
DANIEL. Normal?

(LUKE sits up and looks at DANIEL.)

MILLICENT. *(Glares at DANIEL, then turns towards LUKE.)* I hope you don't mind my asking, but how in the world did you manage to get a bucket stuck on your head?

LUKE. Well, I ... it kind of.... *(Looks to MARGARET and DANIEL for help, but they just look away.)* Well....

(He falls asleep against MILLICENT's chest.)

MILLICENT. Oh my, he's fallen asleep.

DANIEL. He's not asleep. He's just....

MARGARET. *(Gives DANIEL a look.)* Worn out I'm sure.

DANIEL. Right, well Ms. Johnson, if you'll just give me the bucket, I'll get rid of this stuff.

MARGARET. *(Moves U.S.)* That's alright, I'll go with you. I wouldn't want to miss out on a trip to your tool shed. *(Smiles wickedly at DANIEL.)*

DANIEL. Don't you ever quit?

(MARGARET pinches DANIEL's bottom as she follows him into the kitchen.

MILLICENT waves her hand in front of LUKE's face. Getting no reaction, she looks around the room and realizes they are alone. She gazes at LUKE, sighs, closes her eyes and puckers up her lips, as if waiting for a kiss. LUKE opens his eyes, sees MILLICENT, then closes his eyes and puckers up. He waits but nothing happens.)

LUKE. *(Finally)* Thank you for helping me.

MILLICENT. *(Opens her eyes, and embarrassed, quickly*

moves L. on the couch, with her hands in her lap, looking down-ward.) That's alright. You just looked so helpless with that bucket on your head.

LUKE. Oh, yes, I'm sorry about that. I had a little accident.

MILLICENT. Well, I'm sure it wasn't your fault.

LUKE. *(Inches towards MILLICENT and takes her hand in his.)* You know, I really enjoyed cooking with you.

MILLICENT. *(Shyly responds.)* Me too.

(HEATHER enters from the kitchen. LUKE and MILLICENT quickly let go of each other's hands.)

HEATHER. I hope I'm not intruding, but I'm just about done in the kitchen. How are you doing tin man?

LUKE. Very funny. *(Stands.)* but, thanks for your help. I'll just go finish up in the kitchen. *(To MILLICENT.)* I'll see you later if you like.

(He exits to the kitchen.)

HEATHER. *(Sits R. chair.)* Do I feel a little romance in the air?

MILLICENT. Romance?

HEATHER I can see that he likes you.

MILLICENT. He does? How do you know?

HEATHER. Can't you tell?

MILLICENT. I don't know what you're talking about.

HEATHER. You really aren't kidding are you. Good grief, I feel like I've just joined virgin's anonymous.

MILLICENT. What did you say?

HEATHER. I said, we're verging on the amorous. Well, do

you like him?

MILLICENT. Oh, he's ever so sweet. I think I do.

HEATHER. Well, why so glum? He likes you, you like him. What's the problem?

MILLICENT. I don't know what to do. Could you help me?

HEATHER. *(A little hesitant.)* Well, O.K., tell me, have you ever had a boyfriend?

MILLICENT. Well.... *(Pauses and thinks hard.)* not really.

HEATHER. I can't believe I'm doing this. Here we go Millicent, seduction 101. The first thing you have to do is let him know that you're interested.

MILLICENT. How do I do that?

HEATHER. It's the way you look at him. Like this. *(She glances seductively at MILLICENT, looking her up and down.)* O.K., you try it.

(MILLICENT tries to repeat what HEATHER did, but her head movements are exaggerated, and far from seductive.)

MILLICENT. How's that?

HEATHER. Well, maybe with a little practice. Next, as you approach him, use your body language to further attract his attention. Here let me show you. When you stand up, you slowly uncross your legs, then, lean towards him as you gently push yourself upward. Finally, walk towards him, moving your hips seductively, while at the same time keeping constant eye contact. *(Crosses L. in front of Millicent, stops by the L. chair, turns, and with one hand on her hip, strikes a sexy pose.)* Now, you try it.

(She sits L. chair.)

MILLICENT. I don't think my body can do that.

HEATHER. Sure it can, go on, try it. Just remember, slowly, seductively and intent on the prey.

MILLICENT. *(Giggles.)* Prey?

HEATHER. Well, we are trying to catch him aren't we?

MILLICENT. *(Giggles.)* Oh yes, I'd like to catch him.

(She then attempts to get up, uncrossing her legs with a wide arc in the air. As she leans forward to push herself off the couch, she stands up in a very ungainly manner, then moves D.R. to the drinks table. In the effort to imitate Heather's walk she becomes very uncoordinated, and her right arm goes forward with her right leg, while she shifts her weight from the right to the left, trying to get her hips to move. She should look more like a penguin then a seductress. When she reaches the drinks table, she turns, and with her hand on her hip, strikes a pose that is anything but sexy.)

HEATHER. You may need to practice that a little bit too. Now, the final touch is the way you sit next to him.

MILLICENT. There's a special way to sit?

HEATHER. *(Rolling her eyes.)* Oooh yes, and this is what reels them in. You go sit on the couch and I'll show you. *(MILLICENT sits on the R. end of the couch. HEATHER moves sexily as before to sit next to MILLICENT.)* It's really very simple. First, with your feet slightly apart, and your right foot a little in front, you slowly ease yourself onto the front edge of the couch. Then, you run your hand up your leg to hitch up your skirt just a little, while sliding back into the seat. Then finish off the move with another gracefully executed crossing of the legs. As you lean back, place your right arm on the back of the couch, and turn ever so slightly in his direction, gaze directly into his eyes, and smile seductively. Now, pretend I'm Luke and give it a try.

MILLICENT. And this really works?

HEATHER. Trust me. Done correctly, it works like a charm.

MILLICENT. *(Stands.)* Correctly is what I'm worried about. *(Each movement is done individually, with no flowing movement. Turning, she first moves her feet slightly apart in one move, then moves her right foot forward, in another separate movement. She attempts to sit on the front edge of the couch, but misses the front edge and almost falls on the floor. She then pulls herself onto the couch. She has great difficulty hitching up her long skirt, grasping handfuls of material, she slides back into the seat. Her legs then cross, slightly more gracefully this time. In separate and distinct moves, she leans back, attempts to put her left arm on the back of the couch, but accidentally hits HEATHER in the face. She then suddenly leans towards HEATHER, looks into her eyes and smiles a toothy grin.)* I know, I know, practice.

HEATHER. *(Smiles.)* That, and perhaps a change of clothing. *(MILLICENT giggles with embarrassment.)* Did you bring any lingerie?

MILLICENT. I have my nightgown.

HEATHER. Why don't you let me see it?

MILLICENT. O.K.

(MILLICENT exits to bedroom 3.)

HEATHER. Oh Lord, I really didn't sign on for this. If champagne leads to seduction, Millicent is working with lemonade.

(MILLICENT enters from bedroom 3.)

MILLICENT Here it is.

(She hands the nightgown to HEATHER, who holds it up in front of her. It is an extremely unglamorous, neck to toe flannel nightgown.)

HEATHER. Oh my! This is … um … not going to do it. Wait here just a minute. *(Exits to bedroom 1, taking the nightgown with her. MILLICENT takes advantage of the moment to practice 'the walk'. There is no improvement. HEATHER re-enters holding her nightgown. She watches MILLICENT for a moment, quietly shaking her head, then crosses L., and holds up the gown in front of MILLICENT. We see it is an elegant, classy, above the knee black nightgown.)* Perfect, here, take this.

MILLICENT. Oh, no, I couldn't.

HEATHER. I insist. We need to turn lemonade into champagne.

MILLICENT. What?

HEATHER. Nothing. Just make sure you practice.

(MARGARET enters from the kitchen. MILLICENT quickly hides the nightgown behind her back.)

MARGARET. Well, everything is ship shape in the kitchen.

HEATHER. You mean the tin man managed to finish the kitchen without blowing up the entire cabin?

MARGARET. Amazingly, yes.

MILLICENT. It isn't his fault. I'm sure it's hard to be a narcoleptic chef. Will you both please excuse me, there is something I need to do.

(MILLICENT gives HEATHER a conspiratorial wink, giggles, turns quickly hiding the nightgown in front of her and exits to bedroom 3.)

MARGARET. What was all that about?

HEATHER. Oh, nothing really. So Ms. Johnson, we seem to be alone, shall we have another crack at it?

MARGARET. Absolutely, I think we should be fine here. Everyone seems busy for the moment. *(Picks up her briefcase from the L. side of the couch and sits in the L. chair. HEATHER sits on the R. end of the couch. MARGARET opens the briefcase and takes out some papers.)* Now, if I remember, we were discussing the formula to determine the specific dollar amount that the United States government would pay to the Chagos Islands for each barrel of oil pumped.

(Enter LUKE from the kitchen. As the conversation continues, he drops to his knees and crawls under the bearskin rug. He slowly wiggles his way downstage till he is about half-way between the door of Samuel's room and the R. end of the couch.)

HEATHER. I've been thinking about that. I believe it's important that we establish, that if the price of a barrel of oil on world markets rises, then the Chagos Island's royalties should rise proportionately.

MARGARET. I don't see a problem with that, as long as the reverse applies as well. If the price goes down, the royalties go down.

HEATHER. I'm not sure I can agree with that.

MARGARET. *(Controlling herself.)* If you don't mind my

saying so, I find that response to be quite unreasonable.

(Enter SAMUEL from bedroom 2. He trips over LUKE and falls across the end of the couch face down on top of HEATHER's lap as DANIEL enters from the kitchen. He sees SAMUEL, and comes L. behind the couch.

DANIEL. Well, baste my buttocks, and call me a butterball, what have we got here?

(DANIEL exits laughing to the bathroom.)

SAMUEL. I humbly apologize madam. I seem to have tripped over something. *(He bends down, looks under the rug and puts it back down.)* Ms. Johnson, it appears to be your chef again.
MARGARET. What?
SAMUEL. If you don't mind my asking, why is your chef lying on the living room floor under a rug?

(MARGARET crosses behind the couch to the R. of the rug.)

MARGARET. Well…. *(Picks up the rug and looks, then quickly puts it down.)* He's hiding.
SAMUEL. Why?
MARGARET. He um…well, um…he likes to keep a low profile, you know, "BEARly" visible.
HEATHER. It must be "unBEARable" having an employee that's an accident waiting to happen.

(LUKE's head pops up.)

MARGARET. *(Smiling, puts her foot on his head and pushes it down.)* I suppose it's kind of like working with a BEAR with a sore head.

LUKE. Ooow!

(DANIEL enters from the bathroom and comes D. to the L. side of the couch. He smiles at SAMUEL and opens his mouth to speak, but before he can say a word SAMUEL jumps in.)

SAMUEL. *(Holds his hands up, palms toward DANIEL.)* Not a word Mr. Warren, not a word. Ladies, please excuse me. *(Exits to bedroom 2.)*

DANIEL. Has anyone seen Luke?

(MARGARET and HEATHER both point to the rug. LUKE lifts the rug off his head, looks at DANIEL and gives him a little finger wave.)

MARGARET. *(Picking up her papers and putting them in her briefcase.)* Ms. Faraday, let's find a quiet place where we can continue, shall we?

HEATHER. Alright, how about my room?

MARGARET. Perfect.

(She picks up her briefcase and they exit to bedroom 1, closing the door.)

DANIEL. *(Moves R. to LUKE.)* What are you doing?

LUKE. *(Stands up with the rug draped over his shoulders.)* I was working undercover.

DANIEL. What?

LUKE. Yes, I had placed myself in an advantageous place of concealment, for purposes of possible engagement with unknown perpetrators of antagonistic motivation.

DANIEL. What?

LUKE. I was protecting Ms. Johnson.

DANIEL. I give up. You know, you would never be known as the ultimate idiot. You're over qualified!

(DANIEL exits to the kitchen.
LUKE puts the bearskin rug down, as MILLICENT enters from bedroom 3.)

LUKE. Hello. *(Moves to R. end of the couch and sits.)* I was hoping we could talk some more.

(He pats the seat next to him.
MILLICENT comes D. to the left end of the couch, stops and gives LUKE "the look" as taught by HEATHER, but there is no improvement in her technique. LUKE stares at her with his mouth open. MILLICENT then does "the walk" to the couch. Again there is no improvement in her technique, it is still the penguin walk. LUKE watches her intently. She does "the sit" next to him, again nothing has changed. She ends with the big, toothy grin. LUKE just stares at her.)

LUKE. Are you feeling O.K.?

MILLICENT. *(Nods her head yes.)* Oh dear. *(Turns away from LUKE, puts her hands in her lap saying quietly to herself.)* I guess I need more practice.

LUKE. I just wanted to thank you for all your help with dinner. I couldn't have done it without you.

(He suddenly shoots to his feet, motions to MILLICENT to be quiet, and rushes up to the L. window. Slowly and deliberately he goes to place his hand on the window, then suddenly stops and leaps backwards. He looks out, then turns and casually strolls back D. to the couch and sits.)

MILLICENT. Are you feeling O.K.?

LUKE. I thought I heard something, and it's my job to keep the cabin secure.

MILLICENT. But I thought you were a chef?

LUKE. *(Takes her hands in his.)* You are so sweet, I just have to confide in you. I'm not really who you think I am.

MILLICENT. What do you mean?

LUKE. I'm not the chef. I'm an agent.

MILLICENT. An agent?

LUKE. Yes, I work for *(Motions for her to move in closer, looks around and whispers.)* the C.I.A.

MILLICENT. But what about your narcolepsy?

LUKE. All a disguise. I am a highly trained field agent. *(At this point the front door opens silently, and RANGER DON enters. He silently closes the door behind him, and slowly comes D. to the back of the couch, listening carefully to LUKE.)* I am here to protect Ms. Johnson, who is an under secretary in the state department. She has an important meeting here tonight with a representative of the Chagos Islands. We have received information from intelligence that OPEC will make an attempt to sabotage this meeting. My job is to ensure that the meeting takes place without interruption.

MILLICENT. *(Looks adoringly at LUKE.)* Oh Luke, you're a secret agent. How exciting, just like 007. *(Gives a sigh.)*

LUKE. Yes, I suppose I do lead an exciting life. I have been trained so that nothing escapes my attention. I see things that others don't see. I hear things that others don't hear. I operate like an owl in the night, like a cat in the jungle,...

RANGER DON. *(Taps LUKE on the shoulder.)* Excuse me.

(Startled, LUKE jumps up, turns, makes a karate noise and stance, then relaxes.)

LUKE. Oh, it's you Ranger Don, I didn't hear you come in.

RANGER DON. I couldn't help but overhear your conversation. Can I be of any help?

(LUKE moves to the R. end of the couch, next to RANGER DON.)

LUKE. Thank you, but I have everything under control.

RANGER DON. R - I - I - I - G - H - T.

(MILLICENT moves behind the couch L. next to RANGER DON.)

MILLICENT. Luke, you did have one or two little problems outside.

LUKE. Well....O.K. Ranger Don, what do you think you could do to improve the security around the perimeter?

RANGER DON. Well, for a start, I'd get rid of all those ridiculous tin cans and buckets out there. Any fool can see them from a hundred yards away, even in the dark. Then I would place some trip wires, with flares, which I have in my truck. I can do that for you if you'd like.

LUKE. You can do that?

RANGER DON. I can do that. While I'm securing the outside, you can take care of the inside, focusing on all the doors and windows, especially in the rear of the house.

LUKE. Right, I can do that.

RANGER DON. O.K., nobody's getting in or out of here tonight, that we don't know about. Now I've met Mr. Warren, Ms. Johnson and the Reverend. I saw this young lady earlier, but I'm not sure where she fits in.

MILLICENT. Hello. *(Shakes his hand.)* I'm the Reverend Abernathy's secretary.

RANGER DON. Hello. So Luke, is there anyone else I should know about?

(LUKE steps towards RANGER DON and places his left arm around his shoulder. He looks to his right at the same time RANGER DON looks to his left. MILLICENT looks to the right and left, to see what they're looking at. Then all heads turn inwards as LUKE says in a whisper.)

LUKE. Well, there is one other person, whose identity I cannot divulge.

RANGER DON. O - O - O - K - A - Y. Well, we both have things to take care of. I'll keep my eye out for anything unusual. I'll check back in with you later.

(RANGER DON exits through the front door closing it.)

MILLICENT. Oh, Luke, this is so exciting. I thought this only happened in the movies. How do you know what to do?

LUKE. I am a highly trained security expert.

(RANGER DON opens the door slightly and pokes his head into

the room.)

RANGER DON. Aren't you going to lock it?
(He closes door behind him. LUKE moves to the door and locks it.)

LUKE. Right, I can do that. Millicent, I have work to do. There is only one thing on my mind right now and I must take care of it immediately. It is very important to secure the kitchen windows and then check on Mr. Warren's apartment. An agent's work is never done.

MILLICENT. Oh Luke, I'd like to help, but I'm afraid I don't know what to do.

LUKE. *(He takes her hand and kisses it.)* Just relax and leave everything to me. *(Moves towards the kitchen, then turns DS.)* Have no fear, Luke is here!

(He turns and walks right into the wall. He falls, but quickly gets up and exits.

MILLICENT moves D.L., holding her hand to her heart, day-dreaming, and staring off into space.

SAMUEL enters from bedroom 2.)

SAMUEL. Millicent my dear, I really need to talk to you. You need to understand that men are predators, they prey on the innocent. Millicent, please, come and sit down.

(SAMUEL sits R. chair.)

MILLICENT. *(Comes out of her daydreaming and turns towards SAMUEL.)* Oh, Samuel, I didn't hear you come in.

SAMUEL. Millicent, I need to warn you. I am sure that this Luke fellow is not what he appears to be.

MILLICENT. *(Sits couch R. side.)* I know that Samuel, but how did you figure it out?

SAMUEL. Ah, well… the Lord works in mysterious ways.

MILLICENT. So does Luke.

SAMUEL. You must understand Millicent, he's only got one thing on his mind.

MILLICENT. Yes, I know, that's what he told me.

SAMUEL. He told you?

MILLICENT. Yes, he's going to do it in the kitchen.

SAMUEL. *(Stands.)* The kitchen?

MILLICENT. Yes, and then he's going to do it in Mr. Warren's apartment.

SAMUEL. The kitchen? Mr. Warren's apartment? Oh, the depravity of it all. Oh Lord, please forgive me. I have neglected the innocent one entrusted to my care. Millicent, you must not let it happen.

MILLICENT. Oh, but Luke says it's very important that it does happen.

SAMUEL. Millicent my dear, you are in grave danger. You know so little about the ways of the world. I really do not think you know what you are doing.

MILLICENT. That's what I told Luke, but he said all I have to do is relax and leave everything to him.

SAMUEL. The scoundrel! Millicent, I implore you, please go to your room and pray. Pray and remember all that you have been taught, and then practice, practice that which you remember.

MILLICENT. *(Stands and takes SAMUEL'S hands in hers.)* Oh Samuel, such words of wisdom. I will practice. *(Exits to bedroom 3.)* Practice… oh yes, I do need to practice.

(SAMUEL watches MILLICENT exit, looks around furtively, then moves D.R. to the drinks table. He takes a bottle off the table as MARGARET storms out of Heather's bedroom and moves. L. behind the couch.)

MARGARET. Attila the Hun was more reasonable than that woman. *(Sees SAMUEL.)* Oh, I'm so sorry Reverend, I didn't see you.

SAMUEL. *(Caught in the act, turns, and quickly and hides the bottle behind him.)* That's quite alright Ms. Johnson. As it happens, I would like to speak to you about something, which is of the utmost importance.

MARGARET. Of course Reverend, I'll be with you in a moment. Have you seen Mr. Warren?

(MARGARET moves towards the kitchen.)

SAMUEL. Thankfully no. Now Ms. Johnson, it's about your chef. *(MARGARET exits to the kitchen as SAMUEL crosses L. to the fireplace.)* Your chef is a sexual predator who is preying upon the virtue of an innocent.

(MARGARET re-enters from the kitchen and comes D.)

MARGARET. I'm sorry Reverend, what was that? What were you saying?

SAMUEL. Ms. Johnson, may I be frank with you.

MARGARET. O.K., but I thought you said your name was Samuel. *(Laughs.)*

SAMUEL. *(Frowning.)* Please Ms. Johnson, this is no time

for levity. Your chef has said he's going to do it in the kitchen.

MARGARET. Do what in the kitchen?

SAMUEL. Of all people Ms. Johnson, I thought you would understand.

MARGARET. Understand what?

SAMUEL. That your chef wants to take Millicent in the kitchen.

MARGARET. So?

SAMUEL. Surely you cannot condone such behavior.

MARGARET. Where else would they go? After all, that's where all the equipment is.

SAMUEL. What? Equipment! AAGGH!

MARGARET. I really don't see your problem. I'm sure he's just going to give her a few lessons. You know, teach her a few tricks of the trade.

SAMUEL. Tricks of the trade? AAGGHHHH!

MARGARET. Really Reverend, how you do carry on. The kitchen is the perfect place. After all, they'll need room to work. The kitchen table provides plenty of room.

SAMUEL. Oh no, not Millicent, not the kitchen table.

MARGARET. I'll bet they'll have lots of fun. I'm sure Millicent will really enjoy it.

SAMUEL. *(Gives a huge groan.)* OOHHHH!

MARGARET. Excuse me Reverend, but I really do need to talk to Mr. Warren. *(Exits to the kitchen.)*

SAMUEL. *(Pacing slightly.)* What am I going to do? Millicent must be protected from herself. *(Stops at the drinks table, pauses, looks around, then, realizing he is finally alone, quickly grabs a bottle and takes a swig directly from the bottle, puts it back on the table, wipes his lips with the back of his hand and turns D.S.)* Yes, that's it. I must go to Millicent and convince her that this is wrong. I will take her hands in mine and have her repeat after me. *(Enter HEATHER from bedroom 1, she takes one step into the room and listens to SAMUEL.).* I must resist the pleasures of the flesh. My carnal desires must be suppressed. *(HEATHER reacts.)* The innocent physical contact experienced earlier this evening, no matter how pleasurable, must remain pure.

HEATHER. *(Moves D.R.)* Well, well Reverend, I couldn't help but overhear. So, you have the hots for little ol' Heather?

SAMUEL. What?

HEATHER. Carnal desires Reverend? For little ol' me?

SAMUEL. No, no, Ms. Faraday, you misunderstand, it's not you, it's Millicent.

HEATHER. Millicent?

SAMUEL. Oh yes, indeed, Millicent.

HEATHER. Oh dear, I'm afraid she's hooked the wrong man.

SAMUEL. She certainly has, I am so glad to hear that finally, someone agrees with me. Ms. Faraday, may I ask for your help in this situation?

HEATHER. *(Almost to herself.)* Why does everyone keep asking me to help? I guess. What do you have in mind?

SAMUEL. I'm not sure. What do you think I should do?

HEATHER. Well, first of all, does Millicent feel the same way?

SAMUEL. Yes, I believe she does.

HEATHER. And how far has it gone?

SAMUEL. Well, Millicent says it's going to happen in the kitchen.

HEATHER. The kitchen? Way to go Millicent! *(Aside to herself.)* I must be a better teacher than I thought.

SAMUEL. You see no problem with this?

HEATHER. No, there's obviously strong feelings involved, so why not just let it happen.

SAMUEL. No, I can't do that.

HEATHER. Of course you can Reverend. Just do what comes naturally.

SAMUEL. *(Moves U.S. to get his raincoat.)* Really Ms. Faraday, is there no one here with any sense of morality. First Millicent, then Ms. Johnson, and now you. *(Begins to put on the raincoat.)* I shall take a walk outside to clear my head and commune with the Lord, prior to undertaking the task before me.

(SAMUEL is unable to get his second arm in the raincoat because one sleeve is inside out.)

HEATHER. *(Sees him struggling and moves behind the couch.)* It looks like you could use some help.

SAMUEL. Thank you.

(HEATHER sees the inside-out sleeve and puts her own arm in it to pull it out. SAMUEL twists and HEATHER's arm remains stuck in the sleeve. They twist, turn and struggle, becoming ever more entangled in the raincoat. Finally, in one desperate movement, they fall together over the back of the couch, hopelessly entangled together. DANIEL, followed by MARGARET enters from the kitchen. They come D. behind the couch, DANIEL L. and MARGARET R.)

DANIEL. *(Laughing.)* Well, butter my butt and call me a biscuit. What have we got here?

HEATHER. I'll do more than butter your butt if you don't stop laughing and lend us a hand.

DANIEL. The last thing you need down there is another hand.

SAMUEL. Ms. Johnson, since Mr. Warren is apparently too busy displaying his comedic talents, could you please lend us some assistance.

MARGARET. *(Laughing, helps them off the couch.)* Of course Reverend.

(MARGARET turns them around so that the raincoat becomes untwisted, revealing one of Samuel's hands on Heather's derriere.)

DANIEL. *(Points at HEATHER'S derriere. SAMUEL looks, realizes where his hand is and quickly snatches it away.)* I see you've got your hands full, Reverend.

(They finally get out of the raincoat leaving HEATHER holding it.)

SAMUEL. Thank you Ms. Johnson. *(Nods his head towards HEATHER.)* Ms. Faraday. As for you Mr. Warren, why don't you take the nearest elevator, press down, and join Beelzebub!

(SAMUEL turns and exits to bedroom 2.)

HEATHER. Would you please excuse me, I'm just going to go and straighten up. *(Aside to DANIEL as she hangs up the raincoat.)* If you need me, I'll be in my room.

(HEATHER exits to bedroom 1.)

MARGARET. Why would you need her when you can have me? *(Runs her hands down her sides and strikes a sexy pose.)*

DANIEL. *(Leans on the fireplace mantle.)* I told you before, it's not R & R time yet.

MARGARET. *(Smiles at him.)* I like that word, yet.

(She sits in R. chair.)

DANIEL. Boy, you never give up, do you.

MARGARET. Not with a macho marine like you big boy, but I am about ready to give up on the negotiations with that woman. She's impossible. She doesn't negotiate, she demands. She's the most illogical, insensitive, stubborn, unresponsive, inflexible woman on the face of the planet.

DANIEL. *(Laughing.)* Why don't you tell me how you really feel? Seriously though Margaret, I am sure you'll do what's best. By the way, I was wondering if you could do me a favor.

MARGARET. *(Hitches up her skirt and crosses her legs sexily.)* Anything for you my luscious leatherneck.

DANIEL. *(Looking anxiously at Heather's door.)* Pop in and check on Millicent would you, she looked a little upset earlier.

MARGARET. O.K., but then it had better be R & R time.

(MARGARET exits to bedroom 3.
DANIEL watches her as she closes the door, then quickly turns R. and hurries to Heather's door and knocks. He steps back as HEATHER appears in the doorway.)

HEATHER. Did you get rid of her?

DANIEL. For the moment.

HEATHER. Excellent, now we've finally got a chance to talk.

(Noises off from LUKE in the kitchen.)

DANIEL. Shhh.

(They hurry inside Heather's room and close the door as LUKE appears from the kitchen.)

LUKE looks around, creeps furtively to the front door and turns off the lights. He moves to the R. window. He leans forward peering out the window till his nose touches the glass. At this point his body goes totally rigid, he stands on one leg, the other shaking uncontrollably, and his whole body begins to twitch. He emits a bloodcurdling yell.)

LUKE. AAGGHH!

(MILLICENT rushes out of bedroom 3, now dressed in a long, bulky, frumpy robe, runs upstage and takes LUKE in her arms. Immediately she begins to twitch with him. LUKE and MILLICENT continue to yell. DANIEL and HEATHER enter first from bedroom 1, followed by MARGARET from bedroom 3. Lastly, SAMUEL enters from bedroom 2, as LUKE and MILLICENT fall to the floor.)

SAMUEL. Oh no Millicent. Not on the living room floor!

CURTAIN

Scene 2

(Later that same evening.

The drapes remain open, and the couch has become a sofa bed with a dust ruffle and a large comforter. [SEE AUTHOR'S NOTES.] MARGARET is standing by the fireplace, DANIEL and LUKE are sitting at the foot of the bed. LUKE L. and DANIEL R. They are sipping mugs of hot chocolate. LUKE has a large piece of white tape on his nose.)

MARGARET. How's your nose Luke?

LUKE. The outer layers of epidermis were severely burned, but fortunately, thanks to the paramedic kit within my FARTAD, the ointment, which I applied quickly—

DANIEL. She only asked how your nose was, not your medical history.

LUKE. It's sore. *(Stands and collects the three mugs.)* Right, well, if you're all finished with these, I'll take them to the kitchen.

DANIEL. The kitchen? Are you —

LUKE. I can do that.

(He exits to the kitchen.)

MARGARET. Why does he keep saying, "I can do that?" He can't do anything.

DANIEL. He's taking three mugs to the kitchen. What do you think?

(Noises off. The sound of a crashing mug from the kitchen.)

MARGARET. Well, two of them made it.

(Yell from LUKE off stage and then two more crashes.)

DANIEL. *(Laughs.)* What did you just say? Well, there's not a whole lot left for him to destroy, and he's got to go to bed sooner or later. By the way, are you sure you're O.K. sharing with Millicent?

MARGARET. Well, there's only three bedrooms, the Reverend is in one, the Chagos Islands bitch from the black lagoon is in the other, Luke's out here on the couch, so I don't have any choice but to share with Millicent,…. *(Moves onto the bed next to him.)* unless that was an invitation to your apartment big boy.

DANIEL. *(Stands and moves R.)* You are relentless, and no, it was not. Incidentally have you had any breakthroughs with the negotiations?

MARGARET. The only thing we could agree upon was to agree to disagree and try again in the morning.

(LUKE enters from the kitchen carrying his FARTAD.)

DANIEL. Where do you think you're going with that?
LUKE. I don't sleep without my FARTAD at my side.

(He sets it down behind the couch and moves up to the front door and checks the lock.)

MARGARET. I know what I'd like to sleep with at my side. *(Winks at DANIEL.)*
DANIEL. Good grief! Well, let's all get to bed. I'll see you guys in the morning.

(DANIEL exits to the kitchen.
MARGARET heads to the door of bedroom 3, then turns towards
the kitchen.)

MARGARET. You're going to see me before the morning big boy.

(Exits to bedroom 3.)

[See author's notes for the following sequence.]

(LUKE turns out the light and comes down to the R. side of the
bed. He slips off his shoes, then removes his pants revealing
white boxers with red hearts all over them. He folds his pants
neatly over the back of the couch, and gets into the R. side of
the bed.

DANIEL enters from the kitchen, pauses for a moment to look at
the figure of LUKE in the bed, then tip toes quietly into bed-
room 1, and closes the door silently behind him.

MARGARET enters from bedroom 3, with her shoes in her hand.
She tip toes silently R. and exits to the kitchen.

MILLICENT, dressed as before, enters from bedroom 3, pauses
and looks longingly at the figure of LUKE, then exits to the
bathroom, closing the door silently behind her.

LUKE gets out of bed, leaving the comforter so scrunched up that
at first glance it appears to be a person. He then exits to bed-
room 3.

SAMUEL, now minus his jacket and tie, and wearing a bathrobe,
enters from bedroom 2, crosses L. to the bathroom, tries the
door, it is of course locked. Appearing a little uncomfortable,
he returns to bedroom 2.

LUKE re-enters from bedroom 3, sees a flickering light through the window, hurriedly puts on his pants and shoes, goes quickly to the front door, grabs Heather's pink raincoat, opens the front door and exits closing the door behind him.

MILLICENT re-enters from the bathroom, comes down to the back of the couch, looks at what she perceives to be the sleeping figure of LUKE, and comes down to the L. corner of the bed. She takes off her glasses, and puts them in the pocket of the robe. Pulls pins out of her hair, sending it cascading over her shoulders, then slowly and seductively undoes the belt of the robe, slides it off her shoulders, opens the robe, and finally lets it slide off her shoulders onto the floor. She is now seen to be wearing Heather's classic black negligee. She stands for a moment, and begins the routine as taught by Heather. This time everything is right. She slowly strikes a sexy pose, then does "the walk" crossing R. in front of the bed to the R. chair, she turns, gives " the look," and slinks back to the bed. She does "the sit" on the L. corner of the bed, seductively crosses her legs, and smiles at the crumpled covers.

MARGARET re-enters from the kitchen and heads to the bathroom, as MILLICENT quickly ducks down and crawls under the bed, taking her robe with her.

SAMUEL re-enters from bedroom 2, this time he hurries to the bathroom taking little short steps and tries the door. It is locked. Clearly in discomfort, with a little cry of anguish and the heel of one hand covering his crotch, he hobbles back to bedroom 2.

MARGARET re-enters from the bathroom, closing the door and exits to bedroom 3, closing the door.

LUKE re-enters from the front door, the pink raincoat is now in shreds, blackened and burned. He removes the remains of the raincoat, hangs it on the stand and exits to the bathroom, closing the door.

SAMUEL re-enters from bedroom 2, keeping his legs crossed. He hops across to the bathroom door. It is locked. With a loud shriek of anguish he hops to the front door and exits, leaving the door open.

DANIEL, alerted by the shriek, enters quickly from bedroom 1. He is followed by HEATHER. He goes up to the front door, looks outside, closes the door, and switches on the light.)

HEATHER. What on earth do you think that was?

DANIEL. *(Comes D.)* I have no idea, but it looks like Luke is gone, so it was probably him. Would you like a nightcap while we discuss what happens next?

HEATHER. *(Sits at the foot of the bed.)* Definitely. We really need to make a move soon. We can't keep Chris Cole locked in the basement of the other cabin forever.

DANIEL. *(Now at the drinks table.)* O.K. I agree. But when we were hired by OPEC, our instructions were to delay, disrupt and if at all possible, cause the negotiations to break down.

HEATHER. Well, so far I've been able to throw a spanner in the works, but I can't go on indefinitely. The weather has helped, but sooner or later the real Chagos Islands' representative is going to show up, and then what do we do?

DANIEL. Well, you've got her to the point where she's about to break off negotiations. Can you push her a little bit harder? Then we can get out of here.

HEATHER. I can try, but she is one tenacious woman.

(DANIEL hands HEATHER her drink and sits on the bed.)

DANIEL. You're telling me.

HEATHER. If we can just send the Johnson woman back to the state department with all my outrageous demands, it will probably take quite a while for them to figure out what happened. That way we will at least have bought some time for OPEC, which is what we were hired to do. But, what I'm worried about is what do we do if the real Chagos Islands' rep shows up?

DANIEL. If I can get to him before Ms. Johnson, then I think Mr. Cole will have some company.

HEATHER. And if you can't?

DANIEL. Then we'd better get out of Dodge quick. Is the jeep ready to go?

HEATHER. Yes. It's parked behind the other cabin in the woods. By the way, how did you know the recognition code word? Without that, we would have had no chance.

DANIEL. That was a piece of dumb luck. It was the graduate of the central idiots academy who blurted it out.

HEATHER. Well, we've done everything we can for now.

DANIEL. Right, let's get some shut-eye. Goodnight.

(DANIEL exits with glass to kitchen.)

HEATHER. See you in the morning.

(She exits with glass to bedroom1.
MILLICENT comes out from under the bed, and stands in front of it holding the robe, as LUKE enters from the bathroom.)

LUKE. *(Comes D. to the R. side of the bed.)* Millicent, is that you?

MILLICENT. What do you mean? Of course it's me.

LUKE. I'm sorry, it's just that you look kind of different.

MILLICENT. *(Looks down.)* Oh! *(Realizes what she's wearing and quickly puts on the robe and her glasses.)* Luke, sit down, there is something terribly important I've got to talk to you about.

LUKE. *(Sits.)* O.K. Shoot.

MILLICENT. First, what is OPEC?

LUKE. Why do you want to know?

MILLICENT. Well, I just overheard Daniel and Heather say they are employed by OPEC.

LUKE. *(Leaps to his feet.)* What?

MILLICENT. They said they were hired to disrupt a meeting between Ms. Johnson and a representative from some islands.

LUKE. *(Sits down.)* Tell me exactly what they said.

MILLICENT. Well, they've got a Chris Cole locked up in the basement of another cabin. They have a jeep ready to go, and they learned a code word from the graduate of the central idiots academy. What's that Luke?

LUKE. Ah, yes, well... er ... that information is on a need to know basis, and you don't need to know.

MILLICENT. What are we going to do?

LUKE. First, I'm going to capture them, then I'm going to free Mr. Cole.

MILLICENT. You're going to need help. There are two of them you know, you'll need me at your side.

(Enter SAMUEL from the front door, closing it behind him. He comes D. behind the couch unnoticed by LUKE and MILLICENT.)

LUKE. Alright, but no one must know we're going to do it.

(SAMUEL reacts.)

MILLICENT. I've never done anything like this before.
LUKE. You know Millicent, you don't have to do this. You can go to your room right now and lock the door.

(SAMUEL nods his head in agreement.)

MILLICENT. But I want to, I definitely want to.

(SAMUEL shakes his head in disagreement.)

LUKE. Well, I've got lots of rope and two sets of handcuffs.

(SAMUEL reacts.)

MILLICENT. Oh Luke, this is so exciting.
LUKE. We're in this together Millicent.
MILLICENT. So Luke, what's the plan, how are we going to do it?

(SAMUEL silently throws up his hands and exits to bedroom 2. LUKE. goes to the FARTAD and takes out several lengths of rope and two pairs of handcuffs.)

LUKE. We need to get Heather out here first. If you can get her to sit on the bed, I can get her from behind.
MILLICENT. You're not going to hurt her are you?
LUKE. No, I just need to get the cuffs on her. Then we can deal with Mr. Warren.
MILLICENT. Oh Luke, can you do that?

LUKE. *(Looks at her for a moment.)* I can do that.

MILLICENT. Oh, please be careful Luke.

LUKE. I've been training for this moment all my life. I'll hide in the kitchen until you have her in position. Then we'll spring the trap.

(LUKE exits to the kitchen taking the ropes and handcuffs with him. MILLICENT re-adjusts her hair as she goes to the door of bedroom 1 and knocks. HEATHER appears in the doorway immediately.)

MILLICENT. I'm sorry to trouble you, but could you show me "the sit" again?

HEATHER. I suppose.

MILLICENT. Oh, thank you.

(She rushes down and sits on the foot of the bed L. corner.)

HEATHER. Here we go then. Remember the walk. *(HEATHER walks slowly and seductively D. to the foot of the bed R. side and then does "the sit" as LUKE enters from the kitchen with the rope and the handcuffs and comes D. behind the couch. He watches HEATHER carefully, and for a brief moment or two, follows her instructions, and does "the walk" himself.)* Watch carefully now. Remember to move your hips in a swaying motion like this. *(LUKE, now behind the couch sways his hips.)* When you sit, make sure you show lots of leg, and you might even try licking your lips. *(LUKE licks his lips.)*

(LUKE leaps over the back of the bed with a loop of rope over his shoulders and handcuffs in his hand. HEATHER falls back-

wards on the bed and MILLICENT tries to grab her. The three of them become hopelessly entangled as they struggle on the bed.)

LUKE. Grab her hand.
MILLICENT. The left hand?
LUKE. Right.
MILLICENT. Right?
LUKE. No left. I've got it.
MILLICENT. That's my hand.
LUKE. Right
MILLICENT. No, left.

(Finally, HEATHER stands up revealing LUKE and MILLICENT handcuffed together. They are sitting up face to face. MILLI-CENT's right hand is handcuffed to LUKE's right hand with one pair of handcuffs, and her left hand to his left hand with the other pair. HEATHER takes the rope, hogties them together, then exits to the kitchen.)

MILLICENT. Oh Luke, what went wrong?
LUKE. Don't ask
MILLICENT. Has this happened before?
LUKE. Don't ask.
MILLICENT. Does this happen often?
LUKE. Don't ask.

(DANIEL enters from the kitchen on the dead run, followed by HEATHER. He comes D. behind the couch.)

DANIEL. Well, batter my buns and call me a beefcake!

What have we got here?

LUKE. You're under arrest!

DANIEL. Tell me about it.

LUKE. We have discovered you are an imposter. You have been hired by foreign governments to infiltrate this safe house. According to field agent's manual section 33, subsection 4B, paragraph....

MILLICENT. Luke dear, do you really think he cares?

HEATHER. Daniel, I think it's time for us to get out of here.

DANIEL. I agree, *(Turns to LUKE and MILLICENT.)* When you get out of this mess, go over to the cabin across the creek. You'll find Mr. Cole locked in the basement. Here's the key. *(Takes a key out of his pocket and places it on the back of the couch.)* Now, listen up Mr. "I can do that." Section 4, subsection 3b, paragraph 2 of the Marine Corps manual says, "Stay on the porch if you can't play with the big dogs."

LUKE. What?

DANIEL. Don't mess with a marine.

(DANIEL exits front door.)

HEATHER. *(Pauses before following DANIEL.)* Well Millicent, my innocent, it looks like you've got a tiger by the tail.

MILLICENT. What does that mean?

HEATHER. It means you grab it and don't let go. Go for it kid!

MILLICENT. You mean?

HEATHER. Yes!

(HEATHER heads to the front door.)

LUKE. What did she mean?

MILLICENT. This. *(She kisses him.)*

HEATHER. *(Takes what is left of her raincoat from the coat rack and holds it up.)* What the hell happened to my raincoat?

(She exits front door, closing it behind her. Enter SAMUEL from bedroom 2.)

SAMUEL. Millicent, what are you doing?

MILLICENT. I'm practicing the mating ritual of a Japanese bullfighter. What do you think I'm doing?

SAMUEL. Millicent, this is too much! Before you say anything, don't say anything. I have something to say! Millicent, Rome was not built in a day.

LUKE & MILLICENT. *(Together.)* What?

SAMUEL. Oh, that's the wrong one. Millicent, it is harder for a rich man to enter ... no that's not the right one either. I know, I know, something about pearls and swine, or was it sowing and reaping. *(He pauses.)* Japanese bullfighter? I think I'd better go and lie down.

(SAMUEL crosses R. to the drinks table, picks up the brandy bottle, then exits to bedroom 2 closing the door.)

LUKE. Why didn't you ask him to untie us?

MILLICENT. I guess I forgot. And anyway, I'm beginning to quite like it. *(Kisses him again.)*

LUKE. Me too, but look at us, we've got to get out of this.

(MILLICENT and LUKE squirm, and roll over and over to get free of the rope, but are not successful.)

MILLICENT. I think we need to ask for help.
LUKE. I can do that.

(They shuffle over to the door of bedroom 3, MILLICENT knocks on the door with her head.)

MILLICENT. While we're waiting, shall we? *(They kiss again.)*

(MARGARET enters from bedroom 3, interrupting their kiss.)

MARGARET. What in the world are you two doing?
LUKE. Could you please untie us?
MARGARET. *(Begins to untie them.)* Of all the stupid, idiotic things. I can't imagine how you managed this one.
LUKE. It wasn't my fault ... exactly.

(Now free of the rope, LUKE and MILLICENT twist and turn trying to disengage themselves from each other.)

MARGARET. What are you doing?
LUKE. *(Still twisting)* We are attempting to disengage ourselves from our current predicament.
MARGARET. That's never going to work. Where are the keys?
LUKE. Keys?... Oh yes, the keys. They're in my FARTAD.
MILLICENT. Luke, don't be rude, she's just trying to help us.
LUKE. The keys, they're in my suitcase.
MARGARET. I'll get them. *(Gets the keys and unlocks them.)* I can't imagine how the two of you got into this mess.

What is going on?

LUKE. At approximately, 10:23 P.M, I, with a little help from my new assistant Millicent, discovered that Mr. Warren and Ms. Faraday were not in fact who they said they were. *(There is a long pause, and MARGARET waves him on.)* They are in fact OPEC agents sent to disrupt the meeting that was to take place this evening. It appears that Mr. Warren, with the help of Ms. Faraday, kidnapped Mr. Cole and then replaced said caretaker. Only through extreme vigilance and due to my expertise and training were we able to uncover this plot.

MILLICENT. *(Now free of the handcuffs.)* We're going to rescue Mr. Cole. Wait for me Luke while I get some shoes.

(She exits to bedroom 3.)

MARGARET. Where are they now?

LUKE. Ah, yes, well—er—they escaped.

MARGARET. They escaped and you got tied up. I've got the picture. So where is Mr. Cole?

LUKE. He's in the cabin across the creek.

(MILLICENT enters from bedroom 3, now wearing shoes.)

MILLICENT. Let's go Luke.

(She goes to front door and gets her raincoat.
LUKE picks up the key from the back of the couch, and follows
MILLICENT U. to the front door.)

LUKE. Alright Millicent, but understand, when I write my report, you did not see me hanging upside down outside the window, I did not set the kitchen on fire, you did not see me without my pants, there will be no mention of ketchup, I never had a bucket on my head, and we were never handcuffed together. In fact, you were never here.

MILLICENT. I understand Luke.

LUKE. *(Takes MILLICENT's hands in his.)* Thanks for everything.

MILLICENT. You didn't get everything.

(She gives a karate movement and yell, then exits the front door. LUKE turns D.S., gives a " thumbs up" sign to MARGARET and follows MILLICENT, closing the door.)

MARGARET. Well, who would have thought it? Pity, Mr. Marine man, we could have made some beautiful music together. Oh well, *(She pauses and looks at the door of bedroom 2.)* My mother always said, "The best way to get over someone, was to get under someone." Ready or not Reverend, here I come.

(She crosses R. to the door of bedroom 2.
RANGER DON enters through the front door, closing it behind him.)

RANGER DON. Good evening again Ms. Johnson. I'm glad to see you're alone. Now that the OPEC meddlers have left and our so-called security detail is busy for a while, allow me to introduce myself. *(Takes off the hat, undoes some pins from her hair which falls on her shoulders, and peels off her moustache. [SEE AUTHOR'S NOTES.])* My name is Donna Yarid, from the Chagos Islands, and "The Cook Is Awake."

CURTAIN

AUTHOR'S NOTES

PAGE 64: If a football or motorcycle helmet can be fastened firmly inside the bucket, not only will it be much more comfortable, but much funnier, as the bucket will move when Luke moves his head.

PAGE 92: The authors advise against using a real pull-out couch for the following reasons:
>   There will not be time to pull it out and make the bed.
>   There will not be room for Millicent to hide under it.
>   It will not be sturdy enough to support all the activity on
>   page 100 and 101.
Instead they recommend building a platform to rest on the couch, with legs at the foot. This "bed" can be pre-made and placed on the couch in a matter of seconds.

PAGE 94: The authors advise against the playing of any music during this sequence. While it may be unusual to have such a long period of time without dialogue, the silence is what makes it funny.

PAGE 106: The role of DONNA YARID (RANGER DON) has been carefully written to allow the actress playing HEATHER ANN FARADAY to double this role. If this is done, care must be taken to ensure that, when Ranger Don reveals herself as Donna Yarid, audiences do not recognize her as Heather Ann Faraday, i.e. the hairstyles and colors should be very different.

COSTUMES

LUKE JAMES
  2 pairs of tan pants, one wet, one dry
  1 pair tan pants with burned hole in the seat
  Two shirts one wet, one dry
  Two dress shoes & socks, one wet, one dry
  Raincoat
  Raincoat covered with orange paint
  Boxer shorts with hearts
  Shirt and tie with foam shaving cream and red dye
  Burned pink raincoat
  Chef's jacket (or facsimile) and red kerchief

DANIEL WARREN
  Denim shirt
  Blue jeans
  Boots and socks
  Raincoat

MARGARET JOHNSON
  Tailored skirt and jacket
  Dress shoes
  Hose
  Raincoat

REV. SAMUEL ABERNATHY
  White or cream suit
  Socks
  Shoes
  Shirt and tie
  Cape or raincoat
  Bathrobe

MILLICENT
Ankle length dark dress
Boots
Black negligee
Long dark raincoat
Bulky, frumpy robe
Shoes

HEATHER ANN FARADAY
Pastel raincoat with matching hat
Sweater
Jeans
Dress boots
Skirt
Shoes

RANGER DON
Forest Ranger Uniform
Pants
Jacket
Hat
Boots
Rain Poncho
Ranger badge

FURNITURE AND PROPERTY LIST

ONSTAGE

Coffee table
Bearskin rug
Umbrella / coat stand
Sofa
Two low back chairs
Drinks table with bottles, glasses, brandy decanter and bar
    paraphernalia

ACT 1 OFFSTAGE

Flashlight *(Luke)*
Large suitcase {The FARTAD} *(Luke)* containing:
    Electronic bug detection device
    Large cargo net
    2 pairs of handcuffs
    Length of rope
Umbrella *(Margaret)*
Tray with three coffee mugs, coffee pot *(Daniel)*
Margaret's suitcase *(Luke)*
Margaret's briefcase containing papers *(Luke)*
Umbrella *(Samuel)*
Two Suitcases *(Millicent-her own and Samuel's)*
Suitcase *(Heather)*

ACT II Scene I OFFSTAGE

Metal bucket *(Luke)*
String of tin cans *(Luke)*
Crowbar *(Daniel)*
Flannel nightgown *(Millicent)*
Short black lacy nighty *(Heather for Millicent)*

ACT II Scene 1 ONSTAGE

    Samuel's raincoat, on the coat stand, with one sleeve
        inside out

ACT II Scene 2 ONSTAGE

    Sofa bed
    Large comforter

PERSONAL

    LUKE: Wallet with ID
    MARGARET: Purse with ID and car keys
    DANIEL: Wallet with ID, flashlight, key
    SAMUEL: Wallet with ID and AAA card

"SIN, SEX AND THE CIA"
SET DRAWING

TO KITCHEN AND REAR APARTMENT

WINDOW

FRONT DOOR

WINDOW

BATHROOM

COAT STAND

BEDROOM 1

STEP

BEDROOM 3

BEDROOM 2

BEAR SKIN RUG

COFFEE TABLE

FIRE PLACE

DRINKS TABLE

Works by
Michael Parker...

The Amorous Ambassador

Hotbed Hotel

The Lone Star Love Potion

Never Kiss a Naughty Nanny

The Sensuous Senator

There's a Burglar in My Bed

Who's in Bed with the Butler

Whose Wives Are They Anyway?

(with Susan Parker)

Sex Please We're Sixty!

Sin, Sex, and the C.I.A.

What is Susan's Secret?